I0527327

Lemuel Borden

Pamphlets

Lemuel Borden

Pamphlets

ISBN/EAN: 9783337100599

Printed in Europe, USA, Canada, Australia, Japan

Cover: Foto ©Andreas Hilbeck / pixelio.de

More available books at **www.hansebooks.com**

GLANCES AT PAPERS,

CONTAINING

ANALYSIS, INDUCTION, INVOCATIONS

AND

GEM QUOTATIONS

FROM THE

Writings of Lemuel and Emma L. Borden.

1876.

————•••←——

Theophilanthropy and Self-Development,

———O———

It is to love all thought and labor,
It is to love and be a neighbor,
It is to love the present good
Of human life's vicissitude,—
That we, with loving words and REAL !
On joy now paint our loved ideal.

———O———

SEVEN ESSAYS on Health, Education, Religion,

Culture, Labor, Life and Youth.

O read in this scroll
The fires of my soul !
Drink fountains of thought
And live as you ought.
Live, live in the light
And never abuse
The powers we use,
O angel in white!

———

SEVEN POEMS of Love and Life, Sages and Ages, Hymn
to the Greek Goddess of Wisdom and to
the American Goddess of Liberty.

PAMPHLETS,

BY

LEMUEL BORDEN.

If e'er the sacred poem that hath made
Both heaven and earth copartuers in its toil,
And with lean abstinence through many a
     year,
Faded my brow,- be destined to prevail
Over the cruelty, which bars me forth,
Of the fair sheepfold, where, a sleeping lamb,
The wolves set on and fain had worried me;
With other voice, and fleece of other grain,
I shall forthwith return, and standing up
At my baptismal font, shall claim the wreath
Due to the poet's temples.
   Dante's Vision. Paradise, Canto XXV.
See the whole vision be made manifest.
And let them wince whose withers have been
     wrung.
What, though, when tasted first, thy word
     shall prove
Unwelcome: on digestion it will turn
To vital nourishment. The cry thou raisest,
Shall, as the wind doth, smite the proudest
     summits:
Which is of honor no light argument.
     Id. Id. Canto XVII.

1887.

LIST OF PAMPHLETS.

Prospectus, 5 pages, published 1876, containing list of pieces since published, unpublished pieces, and a short poem **not** published **else-where**—"The Christian Home and State."

Essays and Poems, 11 pages. Essays copyrighted in 1872: Health, Education, Religion, Culture, Labor, Life—each chapter condensed into a sentence and the chapters destroyed; Poems copyrighted in 1883: Love and Life, Hymn to Wisdom and Liberty, E Pluribus Unum, Aurora Victora, A Thinker's Workshop, From Youth to Life.

Student and Tribune, Vol. v., Essays, 42 pages:— Government: Methods of Study, "The Majesty of the People", Subjection of Women, Temperance, Puritanism, Strikes, The Curse of the Age, Is there a Remedy?, "The Best Government the World ever Saw", Law for Man and Law for Thing;— "Law": a synopsis including its sources, definitions, divisions, practice theory;— Education: Axioms, What is Teaching?, Common School Idolatry, Examination of Teachers, School Money, Teachers and Teaching, Teachers and Superintendents;— A Freeman's Apprenticeship—Leaflets from a notebook containing thoughts on education, labor, philosophy, religion and literature;- Leaflets, continued;- Wanderings and Wonderings;- An Open Letter to Subscribers to "The Tribune of The People";- Extracts from Tribune, vol. ii.;- A View of The Situation;- Scrawls from the walls of a thinker's workshop. Poems; 12 pages.

A number of "Tribune" vols i. to iv., from 4 to 32 pages.

A Student of English Literature, to contain about 25 pages.

LEMUEL BORDEN, *Attorney at Law,*
Woodstock, Shenandoah County, Virginia,
Began practice in 1878. Collections, a specialty, and money collected promptly paid over. Deeds &c., written. Titles to lands examined. Written opinions furnished. Verbal advice given. Just claims carefully and energetically litigated, and the litigation of unjust claims as carefully and energetically hindered or opposed, when occasions offer. Prompt attention paid to Business. Small fees in cash preferred to larger ones in promises. Business and Business Correspondence solicited. All letters re-

SUPPLEMENT, 3:—Some Hymns of Love in Songs of Life :

> O, for a purer love—a married life ;
> A woman wise and free—Columbian;
> A woman in whose veins there flows and grows
> A revolution, cosmopolitan !—
> Youth and Truth, Two Young Hearts, Meeting, Parting, The Grave, A Tour Among the Rich and Poor, The Sun came up and the Moon went down.

APPENDIX A,—The North American Republic.

> The North American Republic woke
> And thus the genii of her story spoke.
> Columbus said, O, virgin of the west !
> Mine own Columbia, how thou art blest, etc.,
> ——then a description of two historic Americans;
> then Jefferson speaking the Declaration and the Constitution, closing with extracts from Washington's Farewell Address; then Sumner, on the past, present and future of the nation, ending with "the words of our good president," and
> The North American Republic slept;
> It slept, it dreamed, and in its dreams it wept.

APPENDIX B.—The Jews' Theocracy.

> The North American Republic claims
> Maternal care from Jews' Theocracy,
> Whose cherished sons are Russia, England,
>   Spain.
> In ancient Egypt, man was free as wealth.
> Judea strove to make man free as faith.
> The following lines condense prophetic history
> From words of Moses, Jesus and some saints.

APPENDIX C,—The Christian Home and State.

> Throughout the world, the christian homes and states
> Will realize these idealities:—
> Blest are the healthy poor; for homes of bliss
> Are theirs, and states of peace for all their heirs.
> Blest are the meek; for all the earth is theirs.
> Blest are the pure; for joy is purity.
> Such truth and love and worth is happiness.

Behold the shining, shining river,
  The lowly, holy cottage door,
Then tell thy heartstrings as they quiver,
  We're happy, happy, happy evermore.

Here sat the poet in this cell;
Here, learned inspired words to tell.
We'll leave broad acres of the soil
For all the empires of the soul.

November's rain is falling now,
Celestial hands have touched my brow;
Misfortune smiles amid her frowns,
Our tears are jewels in our crowns.
In Fairfield, as in days long past,
My school-boy hopes revive at last,
While the soul of *Burns* is round me cast.

O, come to my wildwood home,
Youth of the starry bright eyes!
O, come to my wildwood home,
And make it a paradise!
I have loved thee long, I have loved thee well, —
I have loved thee more than my verse can tell.
O, come to my wildwood home!

When mine eyes I raise to meet thee,
When I stretch my hand to greet thee,
And with fairest flowers entreat thee,
  Then thou know'st I love thee well.

Your eyes, they are polished
  With heavenly light.
Your name is bedewed
  With my tears in the night.
O, guess not my secret,
  My soul cannot tell.
The angels don't know
  I have loved you so well.
My soul, it is thine
  Where'er thou dost roam:
I will love thee when far
  As I loved thee at home.
Heaven bless thee, dear boy,
  With sweet dreams in the night,
And make thy short years
  Full of heavenly light.

I wish to work and wait, wait and work; work well, wait well, live in peace and sleep with no debt.

> If, like the dial, you will only note
> Those hours your sun has bathed in light and heat,
> That light and life and heat will be your summer day

I choose to grow nearer the ground. I would rather live the lowly life I am now enjoying, with *none* to praise and very *few* to love me. In the narrow vale of content may be found that peace of mind which is dearer than all the praise of a hollow crowd.

"INSANITY?"

Yes! "If madness 'tis to be unlike the world." But good men "keep themselves unspotted from the world" and "the best thing in the world is to live above it."

"And as he thus spake for himself, Festus said with a loud voice, "Paul, thou art beside thyself; much learning doth make thee mad."

No! "I am not mad, most noble Festus, but speak forth the words of truth and soberness."

"His brethren said unto him, 'Show thyself to the world;' for neither did his brethren believe in him."

"Then Jesus said unto them, 'My time is not yet come: but your time is always ready."

"Why go ye about to kill me?"

The people answered and said, "Thou hast a devil: who goeth about to kill thee?"

It is useless to waste words on opponents. Quips, quibbles and quiddities, jokes, items, statistics and prejudices, all enter into the black arm of an influence, which, so far from holding out, we would cut off if we had it. Better, better, a thousand times better, to be annihilated for a day or forever in speaking the truth and doing the right than to be pleased by the smiles of hypocrisy, or the applause of imbecility, or the wages of iniquity: better, than all these, is a sacrifice to intelligence and magnanimity.

GOVERNMENT.
METHODS OF STUDY.

There are two methods of reaching conclusions upon subjects relating to human conduct: 1. The method of observation, comparison, experiment; 2. The method of intuition, imagination, experience. Disputes among scholars and teachers can be reconciled if these two methods by which they reach conclusions are properly considered. Idealists begin with ideas of goodness, holiness, and virtue, and come down to the facts of life and nature. Observers record phenomena and from the connection which exists between causes and effects elaborate the systems of thought and action by which practical men are guided. These observers or scientists have little patience with the worshipers or mystics, as men of practice have with men of theory everywhere. Both methods of study have their advantages and disadvantages; both methods, like all things offered man, are useful if well used. Theories and systems, rightly understood, agree even when seeming most to disagree; that is, when they proceed from honest, sincere and capable persons.

Examine the biography of a man, especially his speeches and journals and letters, and it is possible to forecast that man's views upon every subject relating to human conduct. The conduct of any life and views of human nature and human life depend upon the bias which nature and education give to national and individual character. One person is hopeful, another is despondent; one believes in the efficiency of elective methods, another in prescriptive systems and military discipline.

The safest ground to be trodden in actual life is the middle ground over which aspiration and enthusiastic endeavor may be guided by the milestones of prudence and experience.

"THE MAJESTY OF THE PEOPLE."

When the common people get rid of much of their folly, vice and crime,—then they will practically have right on their side, and as long as they keep skill and right on their side, they will have might to maintain the right. Dream or not! the brotherhood of man and theoretical rights of man would never have lacked power to maintain themselves if wisdom and justice had consented to guide the common people to the oases of civil liberty which existed in the deserts of history.

The great work of heroism has heretofore been the en-
slavement of imbeciles and criminals; it may become
the mental illumination and moral improvement of the
common people in civilized countries and finally the in-
vesting of them with the crown and mitre of a sovereignty which they can maintain by force in every land
and on every sea.

Can the common people free themselves from ignorance
and vice to such an extent that they can govern themselves as well as their governors have governed them?
May not culture and civilization be compelled to crouch
in the holes and corners of dark ages while universal
suffrage is tearing society into fragments with its bloody
experiments?

Aristocracies, monarchies and the demagogues of
democracies are ever ready to take the wages which any
people unable to govern itself can well afford to pay for
good government; but all these governors are so apt to
misgovern, or to neglect to govern: they take the wages
but will not or cannot do the work. Consequently, the
people, dissatisfied with governors and governments, do,
with constitution and guillotine, periodically march into
revolution, and finding their brotherhood-of-man doctrine and universal-suffrage polity as deceptive as human nature is weak,— have only to burn their paper
constitutions and bloody guillotines, and— march out of
their revolutions again.

One sensible thing remains to be done. Every nation
and each individual must prepare for liberty by recog-
nizing the importance and necessity of intelligence and
virtue. No one can learn to swim who is afraid to go into
the water, or has no use of his limbs when he is in it.
When conditions of self-help and self-reliance, self-control
and self-development have been reached, civil liberty and
personal liberty will not long want the power that gives
to life its greatest joy and to effort its best opportunity.
Let man make good use of the liberty any government
gives him, and the times will mend as fast as man can.

But, just here begins the new heroism,— the new monarchy, aristocracy, or demagogism,— because few men,
communities, nations, or ages, will effectually reform
themselves or permit themselves to be educated,— and
only here and there a hero with his band, sect, party,
guard or legion, have the courage and ability to under-
take and make the reforms which are necessary or possible.

A reason why the problem of self-government has
been so hard for man to solve, arises from the fact that
the sciences of human life or human conduct, viz.,
ethics and politics, are not sufficiently enriched by
contributions from the treasures of human thought and
experience. For the same reason that a very good
school is an impossibility, a very good home or state is
also an impossibility. Pedagogy and government, as
yet, have no place on the list of the sciences, and until
the parent, the teacher, and the governor, each knows
what his work is, he cannot be expected to do it.

Brotherhood of man! poet's dream and prophet's prayer! Fountain of happiness! yet some of thy streams have been rivers of death! At last is the doctrine written in the declaration, the constitution and the laws of a mighty nation. What record will the freedom and equality of Americans leave on the pages of history?

Horace Greeley believed in unselfishness. Is it a practical system? Each man to consider the things that make up the welfare of his neighbor? Scattering the springs of human life, character, action, and happiness, rather much. "What is everybody's business is nobody's business." The truth is somewhere between the extremes of selfishness and unselfishness. As the heart is in the middle of the body, away from the extremities, so, the soul of progress, is midway between the human brain and face and hands of radicalism, and the rump and feet and toes of conservatism. Morals are selfishness and philanthropy so mingled as to produce the best result that can be produced.

THE SUBJECTION OF WOMEN.

Hope. idealism, culture, civivilization, and religion, all point to the restoring of humanity or its development, by making the female and the male ct equal parts of the grand miracle of human nature, life and society. "A little child shall lead them." Here is the monarch of the home—a little child. Here is the aristocracy of the fireside—the children that cluster around the hearth of a well-ordered home.

In a well-ordered home the question, Who shall be first in this kingdom? cannot arise. Marriage and private property are two-thirds of the sources from which civilization flows. The culture which arises from parentage is most of the other third. Husband and wife are alike interested in studying and solving the question of the welfare of their children. Reason, experience and love are their teachers— a little child shall lead them.

But despair, reality, ignorance, inhumanity, barbarism and unrighteousness, are the stern facts of life in this world. Wisdom and justice are the offices: where reason and conscience are not, and where sickness, misfortune, pride. fashion, ambition, etc., are, even club law must enforce the demands of wisdom and justice, if no other law can do it. In the slums of the cities and the woodland cabins of the country, and in the hovels of the town and village, woman may be the angel of the household, as she is in the prosperous home every where; but where want and woe are pressing existence beyond the ability for thought, there is little time to argue matters, and no time to follow a ragged, dirty, little child. Is it possible that even under such circumstances, "The man should bear rule and not the woman?"

To avoid such harsh reality and to realize the blessedness of married life under a civilized government, it is necessary that the empire of order, or the rule of wisdom and virtue, should be brought down to a home, a school, a school district, or it might be possible to bring it into most families of a county where the rum shops had been closed fifty years and where honest and efficient teachers and officers had trained a generation and a half so well that men and women and children were anxious to "Cease to do evil and learn to do well." At least every man and woman really wedded, have it in their power to study those precepts and imitate those examples, which, to a considerable extent everywhere demonstrate that wedded love is "the only only bliss of paradise that has survived the fall"— a love that in town house and farm house makes a heaven of its own amid the wreck and ruin that surround it.

But what a man sees is colored by the spectacles of the mind through which he is looking. Some would have woman lead; others would have her to follow, and few are sufficiently wise and good to deserve that they shall go hand in hand, climbing up the hill of life together, tottering down on the other side, and shall rest in peace sleeping together in a grave at the foot of the hill they have traveled over.

TEMPERANCE.

Close the bar-rooms. How? 1. By the legitimate persuasive influence of all the temperance organizations. 2. By teaching in the schools the lessons of temperance contained in the schoolbooks. 3. By teaching from the pulpit the lessons of temperance contained in the Old and New Testaments. 4. By voting every tippler out of office. 5. By voting for local option as soon as public opinion is strong enough to maintain it.

The bible argument for bar-rooms is not worthy of consideration. What fair mind can suppose for a moment that Moses, Elijah, Isaiah, Jesus, John, or Paul, would have spent his days and nights drinking, loafing, cursing, gossiping, and doing the other worse things which are parts of bar-room companionship? The other writers of those books, or the other persons whose lives and labors are recorded in the books of the Old and New Testaments, would, in proportion to their power and influence, have shrunk from such habits and associations. The weakest and meanest of the number could exist in such a company only by preaching repentance to, or laboring for the reformation of, such people as spend their time and money at bar-rooms.

A weak man who attempts to meddle with moral and social questions, does more harm than good. In the first place, his effect upon the world is mere whistling in the north wind. In the second place, by neglecting his own business by attending to other people's, he does harm to himself and family. In the end, it is the world that must look after its weak menders. It requires more wisdom, more patience, more energy, and more honesty and industry and courage, to do a little good, than most schools, sects, parties and persons are aware of.

The army of drunkards is constantly recruited from three classes of people: 1. Those who are *led* into the drinking habit by the influence of luxury. 2. Those who are both *led* by *luxury* and *driven* by *necessity;* 3. Those who are *driven* into the habit by *necessity*— want of proper food, clothing, shelter, and by want of proper social, intellectual and spiritual culture, sympathy, and development. The melancholy result of all these causes of drunkenness is a DISEASE, which is no more a fit subject for ridicule than are rheumatism and consumption.

Recognize the facts of life just as you find them and ascertain their real meaning, but remember that love is queen of life and hope the king of human destiny.

In this age of skepticism, materialism, sensualism and avarice, beyond purifying the moral atmosphere by teaching the virtue of temperance, and the blackboard or other object-lesson teaching, that temperance is a virtue,- included in the workings of License, Local Option, Prohibition, &c.,- any other great result can with difficulty be reached and maintained in practice.

That poverty, intemperance, vice and crime are God's ways of rotting out trash, is a law of nature, otherwise stated, as "visiting the iniquities of the fathers upon the children unto the third and fourth generations of them that hate *ME.*" This law of nature demonstates the danger and weakness of the doctrine of universal and indiscriminate benevolence— that it is as unsafe and wrong to check an individual or race from sinking that ought to sink, as it is foolish and criminal to hinder an individual or race from rising that ought to rise.

The question, "Can we live at all?," is included in the question, "How shall we live?" Duty, well understood, is only another name for permanent and ultimate sucess. As was said by one who not too well understood the science of duty— "I see plainly that if a man will stick to the truth it will carry him out."

PURITANISM.

Cromwell hoped to win England's approbation of the principles which produced and maintained his government. The traditional instincts of England could not thus be overcome. The scholar, the reformer, the writer, the teacher, the statesman, who appeals to the minds and hearts and pockets of a people, can produce gradual changes, but mere imperialism and centralization of wealth and military force, unsupported by teaching in harmony with instinct, tradition, and character,- can produce no immediate revolution in the life of a nation.

Yet genius allied to fidelity to principles which have placed upon genius and effort the crown of centralized power, can do much toward the progress of a country. "As soon as the wild orgy of the restoration was over, men began to see that nothing that was really worthy in the work of Puritanism had been undone." "Slowly but steadily it introduced its own seriousness and purity into English society, English literature, English politics."

STRIKES.

Labor does not know the real value of property. It

will not place itself under the discipline which is necessary to acquire and accumulate property. It embraces another class of influences which fosters all the vices
that degrade human nature.

The foes of the home and of the state are alike licen-
tious, when they strike at Marriage by filling and pat-
ronizing brothels, and when they oppose physical power
and mere numbers to the skill and virtue which have
collected property in the hands of corporations and
individuals.

Strikes, if they have any meaning, can mean only
one thing; this, namely:- Bloated Wealth fosters diseases in the entire social system more rapidly than
Pallid Poverty: Vice and Crime, or Social Diseases,
are what the mills of the gods grind into powder.

After quacks and quackery produced by wealth and
poverty have been somewhat shaken by revolutions,
Marriage, Property and Government will still remain
the prime necessities of man.

Employers and employees, governors and those who
are governed, must exist together, until in some golden
age, man, invested with crown and mitre, shall be
sovereign of himself in *fact* and not merely in *name*, as
he is here and now.

The thing for the friend of the working man to do, is,
plant himself, not blindly against Capital alone,- but
to plant himself squarely against avarice, ignorance,
superstition, knavery and sensuality, wherever he finds
them, and to look for them, first of all, into all the
thoughts and actions of his darling self.

Most persons can do only one thing efficiently, and
yet to do only one thing has a tendency to dwarf character. The Agricultural System diversifies employment by the variety of labor which attends the changes
of the seasons. The Manufacturing system tends to di-
vide mechanical employments by requiring the continual performance of the same work by the same work-
man. The laborer in a factory must expect to find his
services superseded as soon as Capital can transfer his
share of labor and intelligence to machinery provided
by Invention, and as soon as laws of supply and demand
have closed markets for manufactured articles.

If it were possible effectually to restrain what seem
to be the more selfish, sensual and dangerous elements
of human nature, each person might be guaranteed a
subsistence and the means of pursuing happiness, in the
exercise of a single talent. Such experiments have
been made by religious and other communities, but their
success has not been sufficiently flattering to render it
advisable to reproduce them on a larger scale in the life
of states or nations.

The deficiencies,- if there be such in human nature,-
seem but part of the system by which man is surrounded. The envy, strife, struggle and rivalry, which exist
in society, seem to make the feud of Want and Have,

part of the changing seasons and of the various soils, streams, mountains, volcanoes, earthquakes, storms, drouths and climates, which govern human life and destiny. Much may be done by governments, science, art and useful institutions to acclimate man in the earth and bend the human exile to his fate, but all his progress may not remove him from the state of war into which his first ancestors were born, and this state of war may be of the utmost importance to human wellbeing.

THE CURSE OF THE AGE.

The question no longer is, How can a movement against effete authority be started? but rather, How can the tendency of the modern world to destroy all authority, be controlled? Authority, of some sort, must always exist. The nations want fewer political destroyers and more creators. It is easy to unchain the beasts of passion; it is difficult to lead forth the teachers of fact, or draw down the angels of inspiration.

Not the honest, capable lawyer unhung by Jack Cade-ism, nor the small boy with the pistol, is the curse of this Valley. At each courthouse, in nearly every village, at almost every country store, are clubs of lewd fellows who in an atmosphere of profanity, obscenity, tobacco, whiskey and violence, rant about politics. It is the endless grinding of election machines oiled with the deadly ichor of the moral leprosy of these and numerous other schools of vice and crime, that is the greatest curse which angry heaven has sent upon these Valleys, these States, or this Nation.

The most melancholy phenomena which the student of human life in this century cannot avoid observing and reflecting upon, are the following:— A large class of weak persons and also another larger class of stronger persons which includes some of the very strongest characters, endeavor to walk in virtue's narrow path according to the best lights, which are the best printed and oral teaching. With regard to prudence, which has been called "the natural history of the soul incarnate", a prudence which includes in some cases their spiritual as well as material welfare,— in this regard the persons named seem to err as greatly as the liar, the lecher, the miser, the glutton or the drunkard. The error is followed by a penalty which seems entirely disproportionate to the offence which was principally mental,— was the want of perception to discover the weakness of a creed and the folly and danger of attempting too minutely to realize almost any ideals. Each attempt of every idealist to purify himself, places him in the power of the demons who are enslaved to the temporary yet sovereign Fact, and by such demons all such aspiring persons are surrounded. Each effort to benefit said demons results in self-destruction, and each attempt to trust said demons only ends in the betrayal of such idealist, even without the ceremony of the Judas kiss.

Utility, the greatest good of the greatest number, regard for the public good, &c., are in substance identical with the brotherhood of man, human rights, liberty, equality, fraternity, &c., and it is upon this doctrine of utilitarianism, or fraternly, that the whole fabric of democracy rests. This idea applied to societies and nations is nothing more than selfishness or self-interest as contrasted with duty, right, truth, goodness and justice; it is an attempt to govern men by checks and balances arising from self-interest rather than to govern **them** by authority in harmony with the experience of the race and the oracles of the soul. By appealing to universal suffrage, the physical and material elements of civilization mould human destiny, rather than those elements of life and character which are mental and spiritual. Folly fills the throne, hypocrisy covers the altar and iniquity floods the land, with destruction, as really as these results followed in any period that is illuminated by historians. It is the old cry of pleasure rather than virtue, adapted from the beginning of the world to secure the suffrage of the multitude and which always has been followed by national ruin.

There is one truth in utilitarianism: "Physical improvement is the basis of popular virtue." The more important truth, unknown to utilitarians, is, "The kingdom of heaven is within you." Utility and happiness should not be entirely disregarded in the conduct of human life, but narrow is that creed of virtue which shrinks from the discipline of sorrow and the efficiency which springs from a genuine piety. Better is authority with righteousness than liberty with wickedness.

IS THERE A REMEDY?

What are the elements that enter into the idea and constitution of government? Two, only; authority and obedience. In modern republics, authority, in theory, rests with the mass of the people who create executive, legislative and judicial powers which check and balance each other, and all these authorities obey the Constitution and the Laws and amend both according to the dictates of Public Opinion.

The question to be asked is, Can governments organized on the basis of utility or self-interest endure the tests of time as well as those organized upon the basis of duty well understood?

"Forms of government must conform to the constitution of human nature and recognize those arrangements of Providence which are beyond the reach of human control." The Constitution and the Laws have existed from the beginning of the political world in the constitution of man and the laws of the whole physical, social and spiritual system of nature in which he is placed. That form of government which best recognizes and realizes the facts of life and of nature as connected with human societies and individuals, is the best; but other forms are sometimes the fittest, for a given people.

Sparta may have read the eternal verities of political wisdom along with China, Rome, Judea, and the England of William the Conqueror; for Lycurgus through the history of Lacedæmon sent down to this age the unrecognized message, that, Equity, or even justice is equality. A high spirit of ethics and jurisprudence must be sought in the Hebrew and Roman doctrine of duties before rights— the doctrine that was so well illustrated by the Spartan mother, who when presenting the shield, said, "With it, my son, or on it.". Such were the races of ancient times which submitted to the control of reason, justice and the laws of the universe.

"THE BEST GOVERNMENT THE WORLD EVER SAW."

But after the last *vox-populii-vox-diabolii* words have been spoken, the hope of the world may still rest upon the victory of the democratic idea purified from immorality and elevated above its low ideals of common sense.

Is a government by heroes or superior persons, the best government? Is a representative system like that of the United States the best method of securing the services of persons who can and will govern well? Do the benefits connected with our form of government surpass the advantages arising from other forms, and have we now fewer evils to endure than will attend other polities which are possible for us? Upon intelligent answers to these questions, depend the apologies which are so much needed for the factions which have represented the spirit of eleven decades of this Union.

After giving due weight to the lessons of history, allowance must be made for the possible effects of two great modern forces in bringing success to the representative system: 1. The industrial and inventive spirit; 2. The scientific spirit. Also, a third, greater force than all others, seems to be on the side of democratical governments: the course of nature, which appears to be amelioration, growth, progress, development, and the victory of good over evil.

There is a fact deeper than any result presented by the history of man, and that fact is the nature of the human soul. The English people, nation, and constitution, were a growth rather than a creation in harmony with principles already known. Providence controls the affairs of men, and all the builders build more wisely than they know.

The purposes to be accomplished by homes, churches and states, are one and the same:– the cultivation of the pure heart, and the clear seeing eye, and the strong arm. The decline and fall of homes, churches and states, result also from the same cause, viz., the mistaking of means for ends. All domestic, ecclesiastical, and political, sciences and arts which have created the wealth, the fame and the faiths of the civilizations, have, in connection with the sensuality and bestiality of human nature, consumed all human energy, and left the multitude in every age, destitute of the happiness and blessedness which it is the mission of society and government to produce.

The modern custom of reporting the debates and other transactions of legislative and other governmental bodies, and of appointing commissioners and inspectors to examine and report the condition of facts or opinions, and the practice of appointing special investigators to turn mystery to science and of publishing to the world the results of such investigation,- do, by means of the railway, steamship, printing press and telegraph,- enablele the whole people to be present in effect and to assist in the deliberations which precede the enactment, execution, and even interpretation, of laws. This state of things, to all intents, places the first man of the age, whoever he may be,- at the head of affairs; because civilized mankind are now ruled by the spell of a phrase, and from a thousand obscure or illustrious sources may the breathing word be transmitted and the burning thought become a sceptre in the hands of the hero of the hour.

Would it not after all be something wonderful, if after argument and tumult it will be discovered at last that these United States do really possess the best form of government the world ever saw! It is the duty of each generation who inhabit these States to act as if this were true, if the virtue and power of man are all that are wanting to make it true, even if so to act they must believe against belief, hope against hope and love the meanness out of each rascal they run into, or kick countless carcasses of rascality into a ditch, or stand idly by and watch nature make phosphate. Did Horace Greeley speak truths for the next century or millennium, when he uttered sentiments like the following?—

'"With a fervent good-bye to the friends I leave on this side of the Atlantic, I turn my steps gladly and proudly toward my own loved Western home—toward the land where Man enjoys larger opportunities than elsewhere to develop the better and the worse aspects of his nature, and where evil and good have a freer course, a wider arena for their inevitable struggles than is allowed them among the heavy fetters and cast-iron forms of this rigid and wrinkled Old World. Doubtless those struggles will long be arduous and trying; doubtless the dictates of duty will there bear sternly away from the halcyon bowers of popularity; doubtless he would be singly and wholly right must there encounter ordeals as severe as those which here try the souls of the would-be champions of progress and liberty. But political freedom, such as white men enjoy in the United States, and the mass do not enjoy in Europe, not even in Britain, is a basis for confident and well grounded hope; the running stream, though turbid, tends ever to self-purification; the obstructed and stagnant pool grows daily more dank and loathsome. Believing most firmly in the ultimate triumph of Good over Evil, I rejoice in the existence and diffusion of that liberty, which while it intensifies the contest, accelerates the consummation. Neither blind to her errors nor a pander to her vices. I rejoice to feel that every hour henceforth till I see her shores must lessen the distance that divides me from my country, whose advantages and blessings this four months' absence has taught me to appreciate more dearly and prize more deeply than before.'"

Life and Times of Horace Greeley, pp. 248-'9.

The father of the American republic of letters and the finest recognized practical literary genius of our country, said,

"It has been asked 'Can I be content to live in this country?' Whoever asks this question must have an inadequate idea of its blessings and delights. * I come from gloomier climes to one of brilliant sunshine and inspiring purity. I come from countries lowering with doubt and danger, where the rich man trembles and the poor man frowns—where all repine at the present and dread the future. I come from these to a country where all is life and animation; where I hear on every side the sound of exultation; where every one speaks of the past with triumph, the present with delight, the future with growing and confident anticipation." *Washington Irving,* Life and Letters, vol. ii., 242.

LAW FOR MAN AND LAW FOR THING.

Man's best estate is healthy poverty, which means neither poverty nor riches but rather the contentment arising from necessary and unfailing food, clothing, and the lodging provided by a pleasant home which is the property of the lodger. Money in the hands of the best people frequently does as much harm as good and in the pockets of bad people it does more harm than good. Money can keep the moral rottenness from making very rapid progress toward visible decay; but all the money salt in creation cannot prevent a carcass of immorality from putrefying: money rather has the effect of hastening an invisible but stinking and loathsome putrefaction.

Prosperity has more dangers for rational human conduct than adversity. Necessity and the powers that be, keep poor people in their places; but what can control rich people? Only the laws of things—gout, dyspepsia, imbecility and the penalties that follow immorality and vice. One saving feature of democracy is, that it counteracts the luxury and pride which destroyed the old empires which were supported by slave labor. Herein is a compensation, in this, that as much of the starvation and suffering which produce strikes are unusual where slave labor exists, so with the evils of emancipation, pride and luxury are to a great extent swallowed by the sea of democracy.

And now and here come in again with advantage the weakness and even inherent and acquired viciousness of human nature in this, that every human being has an opportunity to live in civilized society. The innumerable wants of civilized man create an innumerable quantity of sciences and arts, each science and each art, like every department of nature, an infinitude in itself. To the hostler who dreams all night about the horse must the lawyer come and inquire if his valuable animal is suffering from bee sting or snake bite; and to the lowest and most brutal bully may that lawyer owe a whole hide if he is caught up in a street brawl.— Persons with little mind, heart or soul, take up their abiding places as the mud-sills of civilized societies. And so there is room for all. The fittest survive and the divine humanity prevents the strong from destroying the weak.

This country as well as Europe is greatly demoralized. Utilitarianism, profit-and-loss, check-and-balance philosophies and the bogus aristocracies which radicals endeavor to reform, rule European and American societies and governments. The result is that the industrious and honest people must maintain those who are idle and dishonest. The fault, dear Brutus, is not especially in our currency, nor in our schools, nor in our churches. As to currency, it is with nations as with individuals. Honesty, industry and economy can stamp their promise to pay on an old hat rim and the promise would not be more valuable if stamped upon gold. As to schools, churches, &c., it is the duty of every practical man who wishes to do no harm, to purify schools, churches, &c., as much as he can, and then to help rather than hinder their work. Character is the one thing that counts all the way through.

Formulas have various values at various times and epochs. The formula of love and humility—or of love and renunciation—was well suited to an age in which the warrior, the miser, the lecher, the glutton and the drunkard were supreme. So utilitarianism, or the greatest happiness of the greatest number, which is but another expression of the preceding formula, may have been the best gospel for England and America which could have been preached during the first quarter, or half, or perhaps the whole of the nineteenth century. These formulas have resulted in democracy and elevated the doctrine of rights so far above the gospel of duty or of duties. In man's passage from the empire of the greatest physical force to the empire of the best reason and truest equity, the instruments of war are gradually laid aside and the instruments of fraud are gradually taken up in their place.

"Forthwith that image vile of fraud appeared,

His head and upper part exposed on land,
But laid not on the shore his bestial train.
His face the semblance of a just man's wore,
So kind and gracious was its outward cheer;
The rest was serpent all."

War is now made by taking away that bread which
the good father holds from none, and hypocrisy and
roguery are the means by which the robbery is now
accomplished.

Not arms and the man, or the sword and spear and
the old warrior,— nor the musket and cannon and the
modern soldier, must be celebrated in the epics of this
new era; nor yet sheep's clothing on wolves—the attempted apotheosis of every form of successful hypocrisy and rascality. No, none of these; but Honesty
and Efficiency maintaining hopeful, joyous, peaceful,
if need be all enduring and all-conquering, and above
all, healthful and loving, life in a modern Home: *this*
is the newer and truer life—or as some would call it,
the religion—and as others would say THE GOVERN-
MENT which the twentieth century demands.

"LAW."

A SYNOPSIS OF LAW will include its sources, definitions, divisions, practice, and theory.

SOURCES

1. In climate; 2. In race and the mixture of races; 3.
In the entire geography and history of nations; 4. In
founders of states; 5. In constitutions, which are either
written or unwritten, simple or complex, but always
the index of the supremacy of one, of few, or of many;
6. In the executive, legislative and judiciary departments of government which are animated by the spirit
and life blood of the constitution; 7. In the religious
or ethical system of a state or people, its conflicts with
material forces and sensual influences, the oscillation of
the human mind between the two extremes of liberty
and necessity which have been registered on the face
of the clock of time and have been remembered or forgotten by history.

DEFINITIONS.

Laws are such formulas for the regulation of individual, social, national and international life and conduct
as have secured the sanction of government. Equity is
that comprehensive soul of justice, which, in the breasts
of judges, governors and legislatures, strives to neu-
tralize the effects of the evil nature of men.

DIVISIONS.

1. Criminal matters and matters of police may be
regarded as the first of these divisions because of their
vital importance to the welfare and even existence of
society. 2. Contracts may next be considered as the
most important of these departments because they

minister to the subsistence, necessity, pleasure and culture of the *individual*. Real estate should perhaps be placed third in the list because its tenure would seem to be intended only to preserve the virtues and **destroy** the vices of the various *generations of men*.

PRACTICE

1. Involves the *examination* of crimes, claims and titles, which investigation requires a thorough knowledge of rights and remedies. 2. Involves or includes the clear, correct and concise statement of the results of investigation in the process, pleadings and other *preparation* of the cause by the judge, or by his clerks or attorneys or commissioners. or by part or all of them; also the summoning of the parties by the court's messengers and similar services rendered by more subordinate servants of the judiciary, which are necessary to mature the cause for hearing. 3. The most difficult part of the practice of law is the *management* of causes by proper use of the instruments of evidence and the oral or written proof of propositions or allegations or their denial, and the eloquence and tact which concentrate every line of law and fact at the point of issue which is tried by the court.

THEORY.

Rules of pleading, evidence, and rules of practice generally, are merely the results of business and of necessity endeavoring to supply actual wants which arise in construing and applying laws; and constitutions and laws themselves are the necessary results which have arisen in construing and applying the reason or verity which controls human society and human existence.

EDUCATION.
AXIOMS.

Nearly all governments take upon themselves the work of public common school education and must stand convicted by the court of common sense and the jury of parental affection if they do not by the most efficient ways and means do two things: first, foster the study of Pedagogics as a science upon which the welfare of the present age and the coming centuries depends; by wise and most practical legislation bring down to the most worthless public school in the most distant mountain gorge the results of this latest and soundest research.

The State says to the parent, "Give me your child; *I* will be responsible for its training." If the state trains up that child in the nurture and admonition of Mammon, Moloch, Belial and Beelzebub, has not that State struck a blow at the family relation; at the foundation of national life and progress? Does it not deserve the curses of a parent's outraged love?

"A Day's Work in a Schoolroom", "A Session in ——
Schoolhouse", or "Experience in the Schools of ——
City", or "County", or "State", have the charm of
memoirs and when they contain truthful accounts of
the actual experience of honest, faithful, earnest, efficient teachers, much valuable information may be obtained by examining them. From necessity, books on
Pedagogics have been mere autobiographies. The
time is coming when these narratives and the essays
and treatises based upon them can be used in the preparation of more scientific works adapted to the actual
school of to-day, to the wants of the age in which we
live, and to the rights and duties and power of that finest of all fine artists—the efficient, scientific, practical
educator.

Among many other important *facts*, parents and edu-
cators should remember the following: 1. All ultimate
responsibility rests upon the government; 2. The educational progress of each nation depends secondarily
upon its subjects or citizens, and upon the teachers
and pupils afterward; 3. The form of school legislation
depends upon the purpose to foster either the political,
military, industrial, commercial, literary, æsthetic, pa-
triotic or religious spirit, or to develop a combination
of all or several of these traits of character; 4. The
character of the teacher is moulded by the doctrines of
liberty and authority which characterize his nation; 5.
The principles of Pedagogy are ground rules upon the
subject of training children in the way they should go;.
6. The methods of teaching result from school legislation, from the character of the teacher and from the
actual state of things in the section where the school
is located; 7. No intelligent and virtuous parents can
delegate to any teacher their entire responsibility for
the life, culture and fortune of their child; and all such
parents who can do so should be the only teachers of
their children.

WHAT IS TEACHING?

The invention of printing has revolutionized all teaching to such an extent that the real university is a col-
lection of good books. The living voice of the teacher
is mainly valuable for the exalted character that is behind it. Teaching is not now the imparting of knowledge; it is the imparting of a healthier, stronger and
purer selfhood to the physical, mental and moral constitutions of children by teaching them to read in printed books and in the volumes of nature, of life and of
the human soul. The criterion of all good teaching is,
that a pupil begins this course of reading when a little
child and pursues it with delight and with a view to
the proper conduct of life so long as life lasts.

"Education is formation, rather than information;"
it is the development of healthy, intelligent, and above
all, virtuous, manhood and womanhood; it is the "ac-
quisition of physical, mental and moral power by self-

development and voluntary effort"; it is communing
with nature face to face in solitude and profiting much
by all the lessons of life's great school which society
can offer.

"Delightful task! to rear the tender thought;
To teach the young idea how to shoot;
To pour the fresh instruction o'er the mind;
To breathe the enlivening spirit and to fix
The generous purpose in the glowing breast!"

COMMON SCHOOL IDOLATRY.

There is an idolatry which is injuring the common
school system of this country—a useless and harmful
worship of old intellectual forms which though sanc-
tioned by tradition have long since lost much of their
value. This ancient idol worship is joined to a modern sort which worships penmanship, map drawing,
mathematical, historical, orthographical, elocutionary
and other puzzles and numerous new mechanical and
intellectual forms which never possessed the value or
significance which has been attached to them.

In the place of this worship of grammar rules, this
parsing, analyzing, counting, reading and reciting by
machinery, is needed a theory and practice of teaching
from which correct speaking and writing will follow
naturally from pure and sincere thinking and acting; a
theory and practice of teaching which allows character
to control handwriting and already sees a possibilty of
dispensing with penmanship to a considerable extent
by means of type writers, small printing presses and
other machinery to be supplied by invention; a theory
and practice which wastes no time and energy in mem-
orizing insignificant dates, names of sham heroes, un-
important places and of events not worth remembering
whilst the important results of history, hygiene and
morals, and the master-pieces of literature, are unknown
or unnoticed.

What is needed most of all for the common school
system of the United States is more and more genuine
literature—literature which is the expression of real
heroism and genuine patriotism, and of human excel-
lence derived from the experience of all the ages and
specially adapted to the special demands of the present
age and our own nation. A man or woman competent
to form the minds of youth in harmony with the virtuous precepts and examples which should be included
in a better body and soul of literature than has yet been
presented to the public in any series of school readers
—s u c h a man or woman who is willing to wait for
praise beyond monthly reports and examination days
until the honesty and efficiency of coming years of
well-spent life shower blessings on the true teacher's
head—is worth a million of those educational quack s
who to a little parsing, analysis, cube root, a few maps
drawn, a little slow penmanship and a few names in

history and geography, and some long words from the dictionary, and much of Scrapewell's stingy philosophy or the practices of the debauchee,— add a life of dishonesty, inefficiency and shame on the parts of both pupil and teacher as a fitting commentary on the old text: They who sow the wind shall reap the whirlwind.

EXAMINATION OF TEACHERS.

Cæsar's soldiers were sure that after every battle each soldier would receive that promotion which he earned and deserved. Likewise, it is only in the heat of the contest of actual school work that the lieutenants of superintendents of schools can be selected with accuracy. But then before the genuine teacher can be seen, the eye of a teacher is as absolutely necessary as is the eye of a soldier to the selection of a soldier.

The mistake of the examination paper system is, that four of the most important qualifications of a teacher are sacrificed to a fifth which is practically of minor importance, because the want of this fifth qualification can be detected even by a quack, while the other qualifications require the eye of a hero and an expert to discern their presence in and absence from the work of the teacher. No teacher can stand the fire of pupils and parents, trustees and fellow teachers, the public, the county superintendent to whom he must make monthly reports,– without exposing his ignorance. The other four of the most important of the teacher's qualifications are mental capacity, moral character, teaching power and governing power.

The disadvantage of the examination paper system is, that it furnishes data which readily adapt themselves to calculations in percentage, and which can be tied into bundles with red tape and paper strings. A great evil connected with the examination paper system is, that in the hands even of an extraordinary superintendent the school system of a county is apt to run to red tape, or paper strings, and in the hands of ordinary superintendents it always does so.

SCHOOL MONEY.

If the schools were taken away from politicians and sectarians, scoundrels and dandies and imbeciles, speculators and Scrapewells, and managed as a great private enterprise is managed—a railroad or a cotton mill —better work would be done at 75 cents a day than is now done at $1.50 a day. The officers should form simply the muscles or the administrative part of the organism and some competent expert in pedagogy and public education should furnish legislators and educators with the indispensable brains or science which is the soul of an educational organization. Not great salaries, but better legislation, organization and administration are wanted. Make better use of the money you are already spending. Above all, know the precise

18

purposes for which *our* public schools exist: 1. To
make free government possible by making *good* citizens;
2. To enable each pupil to make an *honest* living and
to live a useful, happy, efficient life. To accomplish the
first purpose, the teachers and school officers and all
intelligent and virtuous parents, must be intrusted with
power similar to that which republican Rome gave her
censors *morum*. To accomplish the second purpose, the
best male and female—and as soon as possible female
—character in the country,- that which has grown in
the cleanest, strongest, most useful and most happy
homes, with little knowledge of or respect for, ordinary school, college and university qualifications;- s u c h
character should in the schoolroom mould the character of youth.

It is verily "more blessed to give than to receive,"
for the excellent reason that no man, woman, nor child,
saint, sinner, demon, nor angel, can receive charity
without suffering degradation. The fact that many
people are compelled by their nature to refuse the assis-
tance they solicit, explains the inefficiency of many elee-
mosynary institutions, and the same fact also accounts
for much social and individual ingratitude.

The effect of money upon teachers is the same as on
other officers, and the reason is that real teaching and
real governing are work that never has been and never can be paid for in money. Yet for the sake of money any field will be filled to overflowing, and it is for
the sake of pay in dollars and cents and for that cause
only that there are more teachers than schools and
more applicants than offices. If this scramble for money ended in genuine education and in good government
no true man would envy teachers and politicians their
bed and board; but the result of this scramble for office
is misgovernment, and the result of the millions spent
for education seems to be new and more dangerous
forms of vice, crime, disease, and learned ignorance,-
all of which, like all old and new forms of sin, are a
reproach to any people. "Righteousness exalteth a nation."

TEACHERS AND TEACHING.

There are two theories and practices of teaching; the
one is lifeless, soulless and mechanical; the other is intellectual, moral, spiritual, living and life-giving.

What *is* the child at the end of a session, and at
the end of his thirtieth or fiftieth year? and not what
few grammar and arithmetic rules he has memorized,
is the important question.

The true teacher may use neither a parsing nor a
counting machine, but the pupils will learn kind, correct,
elegant and courteous expression from his own lips,
and correct speaking and writing will follow naturally
from the pure, strong and beautiful thoughts which the
true teacher rears in every pupil's mind.

The true teacher would with Dr. Ruffner, the first State Superintendent of Schools in Virginia, turn attention to hygiene, morals, manners, good reading, good spelling, and especially to the development of gentle, honest, industrious character.

The reading lessons are the soul of the school.— Take an extract from the Bible, from Shakspere, from Milton, from Dr. Johnson, from Addison, from Carlyle, or from our own Emerson. Few of the most intelligent and aged saints who have made the Bible a lifelong study can impart the lesson of a sentence to a young mind,— or rather awaken the sleeping germs of virtuous character. The same thing is true of an extract from any of the numerous writings mentioned; because as an eminent and learned man once said, "It takes all I know and more than all I know to make even the commonest things plain to the minds of young people." How much more difficult is it to gather the pearls of modern wisdom from modern seers and with them evolve the ray of genius which is struggling within the pupil's being to become the light of his life? And yet here is almost nine-tenths of the teacher's power as schools are now constituted. To teach on this theory, education, like divine religion, is a kingdom that "cometh not by" nor with "observation". Like the true preacher the real teacher aims at the conduct of life and he dreads the anger of his God and the upbraidings of his conscience more than he loves the dollars or the praises of men.

An extract from a book in a reader is like a single nut from a tree, or an ear of corn or a head of wheat from a grain field. To know anything of the crop or to get any benefit, you must know the tree or the field and possess more than a single nut, head, or ear—that is, you must know the source or the author and be familiar with the writings from which the sample has been taken. Very frequently, owing to the stupidity of the public and the avarice of compilers and publishers, the particular nut, head, or ear, is small or even rotten. Yet the whole field of wheat is to be judged by this sample,— all the wisdom of a gifted personage is to be extracted from a single sentence or from a few paragraphs,— and THE teacher(?) has never before heard of the author's name and knows nothing of his thirty or fifty volumes which alone would require five years' study. The *real* teacher has studied the life and the system of thought out of which the author and his writings grew, and best of all he sees in each good author the images of truth and holiness which are mirrored in the crystal streams of his own shining life. Such a teacher and his pupil can see the oak and the hillside where the oak tree grew—they see in the extract the writings and the age and society in which the writer lived and labored and the relation of the same to other writers, other times, and other places.

But you have only the nut, the tree rather or the plant on which the grain or the nut has grown. The fruit must be severed from the plant on which it has grown. This is calling or correctly pronouncing the words represented by the oil and lampblack on the printed page. The word has not yet been made flesh; sound has been made of it, rather: the nut or the grain has been severed and now lies upon the surface of the earth: the thought has likewise been severed from the plant whereon *it* grew and *it* lies on the surface of the mind.

What is breaking the bur or hulling the walnut? Defining the words. What is breaking the walnut or biting open the chestnut when they have been taken out of the hull or bur? That is defining the extract and gathering the seminal thought from the words and forms by which it is encumbered.

But as yet we have had no food for body or mind. The kernel must be chewed, swallowed, digested, and what the system refuses must be cast out again from the mind as well as from the body. A selecting memory is often more valuable than a retentive memory, and as different persons crave different kinds of food for their bodies, so all minds cannot be fed upon the same kind of grain or kernel, even.— What we oppose is this indiscriminate cramming of worthless formulas; this feeding of chaff, husks, hulls and burs to young people.

Now this supervision of the teacher in obtaining the kernel from the tree of knowledge and intellectual and spiritual food from the seed-field of time, this chewing and swallowing and digesting of the intellectual and spiritual fruit, or grain, or kernel, of a literary master-piece,- by the pupil;- require from the teacher no more and no less than the shaping of vessels unto honor and dishonor at his own will. The skillful teacher by thus properly teaching these reading lessons, and by concen-trating more time and effort upon them, has it in his power to mould the morals, manners, health, fortunes, and to a great extent the character of his pupils; because as really as the lesson about the lark and the farmer teaches the pupil that he should do his work himself, so every extract not designed merely to please or amuse should have a tendency to influence the conduct of life until the boy or girl has crossed the meridian and passed the sunset of existence, to the end that the child, hav-ing done its duty and its work, shall, in the full-ness of years, come in peace to his grave, as a shock of corn in his season.

TEACHERS AND SUPERINTENDENTS.

I know of no first principle in education, nor second, nor third, unless they are something like the following:
1. Let the teacher conscientiously earn every cent he draws from man's treasury and religiously endeavor to

deserve additional **wages** to be paid—(as such wages always are paid. with compound interest,)— from God's exchequer. 2. Not knowledge but character, is the beginning, the middle, the end: "not how the universe was formed but how we may pass through it in safety." 3. The schools were made for the children; not the children for the schools.

Competent and faithful superintendence is the soul of the public school system. There is yet no science of the Supervision of Education by the civil authority. If such a science is formulated as it should be formulated in a government like ours, its first three principles will be:— 1. The best bodied, best brained, best cultured and best paid man in the nation, state, county, city, township, or district, as the case may be; 2. Faithful, impartial, continual, sympathetic, and complete, study of subalterns and of the sections and material upon which subalterns are working to the end,— 3. That each act and utterance of the superintendent may be the word which should be spoken and the act which should be done.

But the real teacher is the intelligent mother, and the genuine superintendent of schools is the father who in the vigor of

"Manhood looks front with careful glance."

A FREEMAN'S APPRENTICESHIP;
LEAFLETS FROM A NOTEBOOK
Containing Thoughts on Education, Labor,
Philosophy, Religion, and Literature.

Elementary and university training should have the same object in view—the growth of character by means of self-culture and self-development. The results of all teaching should be efficiency and happiness and the performance of duty in the department of labor and position in life for which the individual is best suited. In the work of education and in the work of life, four things should be constantly kept in mind:— 1. Good Health is the matter of primary importance; everything else is of secondary importance; 2. To promote good health some Private Property is absolutely necessary and too much is absolutely injurious because riches frequently hinder that mental and spiritual labor and exercise which is the law of health, growth, culture and development; 3. In connection with rights to private property, love for and loyalty to Woman, and the Institution of Marriage, and the relation of Parentage, are the strong forces which civilize nations and perfect the character of individuals; 4. Upon this basis of Health. Property, and Marriage, rests every form of *Ideality*, or what is commonly called culture and education—Art, Science, Literature. Morals, Religion.— The error alike of university and elementary training is the hypothesis that culture can be imbibed by studying printed books several years. The fact is, genuine culture can be gained only by healthy growth in wisdom—by a healthy life of honest Labor which reads the Book of Nature in the School of Experience.

There should be consolidation of the Teaching Services, because like all other sciences the Science of Human Life is interlocked and intertwined not only with almost every science but also with almost every art. The teacher's preacher's and professor's Teaching Services,— the Teaching Service of the publisher, editor and author,— that of the lawyer and the doctor,— the Teaching Services of the farmer, mechanic, manufacturer, inventor, and merchant, should be consolidated into one grand Apprenticeship pointing toward the degree of Master and Mistress of Arts, and Husband (not Bachelor) and Wife of the Science of Life,— a science which embraces all knowing and doing in the single art of Virtue or Manhood and Womanhood during the periods of childhood, youth, and age. This Apprenticeship should embrace as much as each person needs to begin with and enough to go on with and end with in the work of self-help, self-culture and self-development. Such an Apprenticeship is life in the British and German empires and in the French and American republics to all who are wise enough to choose the end and strong enough to use the means.

Too much of the sand of deceit is used in all the trades, professions and occupations. A certain amount of knavery and imbecility will exist in society as a carcass upon which the eagles of force and the buzzards of fraud can gather, but there is no use that every man forever considers the public a goose and anybody a fool who will not pick her. Many trades and professions have been almost entirely revolutionized and many new ones have been created by the progress of education and invention,— by means of labor saving machinery, &c. Many old trades and professions will go on under new forms and names, but the model American citizen will consolidate many of them into a single Teaching and Working service which any wise, strong, true, man, and loving woman can realize in a home of their own which is built upon their own land.

As Hints for Apprentices who wish to become journeymen, and for Masters and Mistresses of the Science of Sciences, and Husbands and Wives of the Art of Arts, the various departments of Thought and Labor should be carefully examined and their worth and worthlessness in the free man's, or true man's, or wise man's, or good man's, or noble man's, or pure man's, or healthy poor man's and meekly valiant man's home, should be clearly pointed out. Such is the purpose of many of these "Leaflets."

The people can never know their benefactors. This is better for the benefactors and the people too. It is better for the benefactors because the difficulties with which people surround them are their best discipline, and too much recognition would cause said benefactors to enjoy the fruit of their labor and not be instant in season and out of season. It is better for society because the sum total of moral vigor in the world is thereby increased.

· The fact that a public servant or a true, honest private individual, is under the heels of the people, is a point in his favor. Let your universal suffrage winnowing machine be perfected by the township system and a thousand dollars above expenses in the treasury of the school district. Let that be done if you can do it. So far as I am concerned, I remain neutral during such effort, but I watch the experiment with intense interest. The result is clear. Unless you can reach the time when every muscle worker shall be able also to be a brain worker and thereby destroy the necessity for professional brain workers, there must be ten or a hundred muscle workers for one brain worker. The additional facts that efficient brain work requires a lifetime of systematic effort directed to a single point and the support of thousands of dollars and the best natural ability,- raise doubt that health, knowledge and virtue can ever cover the earth as the waters cover the great deep. Can the people know their benefactors until after they have killed them? Is it probable that mankind will go on refusing to be educated in the real sense of the word—refusing to be healthy, intelligent and and virtuous?

A neat, good schoolhouse, even in Old Virginia, is a telescope which discloses much that the future hath of marvel and surprise. If our civilization does not contain within itself the germs of its own destruction, the real captains will step to the front under all hindrances and master us by some fair means. Recognized or unrecognized, the world's benefactors will heap up benefits for human-kind. The progress of the past two hundred years which has followed the last awakening of the human mind, may continue to destroy some professions and create others, until the necessity for walls of separation between brain workers and muscle workers will be lessened until the necessity and the walls and gulfs of separation themselves will pass entirely away in the healthy, intelligent and virtuous character of human beings who inhabit this earth in the near or distant eons.

A Domestic Science will yet include all the sciences. Each ray of wisdom and knowledge should enlighten the mind enliven the heart and nourish the character of man, woman and child, as really as their bodies are nourished by food prepared at the domestic hearth,- as really as the members of the household are warmed at, and the domestic circle formed around, the home fireside. Halls of learning and of justice and temples of religion, are sparks from the fire which the savage kindled to warm his limbs and cook his scanty meal,—and learning, joined to genius and virtue—or wisdom—is the torch of human liberty lighted by sparks from that primitive hearth—liberty which proceeds from wisdom and represents all the strength expended by man in struggles with such forces of nature as man can conquer.

As all sciences are contained in the science of life, so all arts united constitute the art of living. Every trade and profession and occupation must bring its choicest offerings to the sanctuary of home. Teachers, preachers, editors, authors, lawyers, doctors, inventors, discoverers, mechanics, manufacturers, merchants, agriculturists—all the sciences, arts, culture and progress of civilization, exist to adorn the home of civilized man, and are clumsy agencies and nothing more by which the well-ordered home is supplied with food and raiment, fuel and shelter, for body and mind,— and the germs of them all exist in the mind of every healthy, intelligent and virtuous father and mother, daughter and son. All human achievement is the gift of the race to the individual and of the individual to the race.

How naturally does all human thought and action, being and becoming proceed from marriage and private property—radiate from and again concentrate in this fire from the fireside! Teachers, preachers, lawyers and doctors, editors and authors, are only peddlers of a few short rules for the well-being of the minds, bodies and pockets of civilized man—they are wandering ballad-singers, beggars on the highway of life, who retail a few short poems which with difficulty enough they have grown old in learning from books and institutions which contain light caught from the countenances of all the shining ones who have lived on the earth. All the labor and learning of inventors, discoverers, mechanics, manufacturers commercial men and agriculturists, exist but to provide an ear for the ballad-singers aforesaid.

A strong, true man, and a true and loving woman, in an American home on their own land, can provide such an ear. Can they not sing their own ballad? Or better still, they can feel the burden of the earth's song through all ages since the first savage kindled the first fire and with that fireside began the establishment of arts and sciences, laws and customs. And, best of all, can such a man and such a woman rise in the strength of manhood and the beauty of womanhood, and with voices in such harmony as the ages never heard, raise a song more melodious than the shining ones have sung.

Here is the glory of the home, and in a home such as this is the battle ground upon which human nature will yet gain greater victories than are now recorded in the annals of the human race.

As guide-posts on the highway of progress which leads to this victorious warfare, the writer of these lines has endeavored to obey three "Humane Laws": 1. Leave

no vile men, women and children on your path of life;
2. Earn more than you use and use no more than you
need; 3. Rule your own household as well as you can,
but (if the interests of good order will permit), Rule
none and be ruled by truth, worth, love.

LEAFLETS.

1. All sects, parties and human institutions exist for
man's benefit, and if he permit himself to exist too long
for their benefit, life's error will be the want of a little
independence, self-reliance, and originality.

2. These orators and politicians will bring fire down
from heaven or up from hell to bake any loaf of bread
which is ready for their oven. No importance can be
attached to any of their words or actions. Now, as
ever, the nod of an honest man, or a shake of the head
which is a good man's commentary upon their lives,
labors and characters,- is of more value to the people,
whom these orators are continually using as cat's-paws,
than all the speeches and editorials that have ever
been crammed with deceit.

3. As a class, the lawyers of Virginia, have been,
during the last ten years, systematically persecuted.
If this class contains much of the gold of character, it
will come out of the furnace refined and purified, and
as it regains power and prestige, it will promote the
welfare of Virginia. If the profession is indeed composed principally or entirely of scoundrels, the furnace
of persecution may yet be heated seven times hotter for
its benefit.

4. The man who walking the narrow path and enter-
ing at the straight gate stands alone from the necessity
of his situation,- is in danger,- because, like all mortals,
in the midst of life he is in death: but he who travels
the broad road and enters at the wide gate of destruction, and like a piece of drift-wood is borne on the
waves of the crowd,- is in greater danger than he who
stands alone—than he who is

"Beset
With foes for daring singly to be just,
And utter odious truth."

Intellectual and moral forces rule this world and not-
withstanding the chuckle of success which proceeds
from well fed parasites in home, church, school and
state,- coarse materialism, however well presided over
by low cunning and fortified by the weak strength of
lower rowdyism,- can never reach the height, the depth,
the length, the breadth, of beatific, inextinguishable, all-
conquering being.

5. "What have you accomplished by your elaborate
opinion? You have unsettled everything; settled nothing."

Many questions admit of no other treatment in the

present state of knowledge. Of this class are questions of casuistry, ethics, pedagogics, and numerous similar branches of knowledge which result from new phenomena presented by American life and American society. *Any* **treatment** of these subjects which is marked by **vigor and originality**, is preferable to **Old World** dogmatism **and the fitting** of worn-out formulas **to new and** living societies. **What** many people **need is not** information, but conviction of their ignorance. Such people's false views must be unsettled before true views can be settled for them.

6. The best and even richest newspapers are those which rise above slavery, bigotry and imbecility, and give both sides of a question with such force and originality that even governments must bow the ear to listen, and then must act in accordance with what the able editors have told them is the truth. The best test of scholarship is declared, even by some leading universities, to be, ability to prepare disquisitions upon subjects of human interest—ability to see both sides and all sides of a question as clearly as any and all **partisans can see;**- for only by this method are complete views attained: and the modern world demands the many-sided, myriad minded man.

7. The first and most fundamental principle in the theory and practice of law, medicine and theology, as these sciences (?) and useful arts should be practiced, are the same: as little of each as the imbecility, crime and disease of the people will permit. The same fundamental principle is true of the sciences of ethics, politics and pedagogics, and the numerous other arts, professions and vocations based upon the sciences last mentioned. The ignorance embraced in the no-knowledge and half-knowledge connected with these subjects is best neutralized and banished by a simple, unbiased study of the most obvious facts connected with these departments of thought and action;- and genuine skill will result from the patient, careful application of the results of such study to the work in hand.

8. Not altogether the greatest happiness of the greatest number,- but also the most exalted virtue of the greatest number, or even of the few who live in Edens far apart,- the safety of the greatest number, and especially of the few whose safety is most important to the state, and the obtaining of much needed speedy justice —capital and other punishments—by the greatest number of Judases, as well as justice for the Socrates whose sentence should have been, "Maintained in the Prytaneum at the public expense because he deserved well of his country,-" and the development of genuine manhood and womanhood by the greatest number and by the best quality.- and the realization of the best ideals which are in accord with **the** objects of human

existence—these things and such as these, are **bases** upon which the fabrics of government rest.

9. An action is just and right not because it harmonizes with any hard and fast, cut and dried, theory, but because it represents the strong, and kind and pure human soul, and the divine soul as evidenced by the best books and institutions; because it is in harmony with the holiest living forces around us and with the holiest living forces within us; and because such action even aspires to be in harmony with the system of nature or of the universe, of which we, and the earth, and our solar system, are an insignificant fraction.

10. Temperance, Industry. Economy, Intelligence, Self-reliance, are essential parts of the moral system or system of morals or ethics which America needs.

11. There is some of the imbecility of egotism, and of the immorality or of the crime of suicide,– in martyrdom. The great superiority of Shakespeare over Moses, Lycurgus, Cæsar, and other eternal names of fame, is, that Shakespeare earned a home, planted trees and passed his old age with his neighbors and friends, and died at home in his bed, careless if not ignorant of the fact that he is the height of the human race.

12. The labor problem is unsolved; perhaps it is unsolvable: it is a sphinx riddle bequeathed by the ancients to the moderns, by the old world to the new. Man is now emancipated and he finds his freedom simply freedom to die by starvation. The industrial systems of the age are so many Columbuses in a few tubs at the port of Palos in Spain, ready to sail over unknown oceans to an unknown world. The old civilizations were based upon slave labor which is but the Greek, Roman, and Oriental mariner, proud that his clumsy craft can sail on the Mediterranean pond. But eastward over the Pacific and westward across the Atlantic of science and civilization, must the crews of the Santa Maria, the Pinta and the Nina again come bearing the new social, political and religious Columbus to the new industrial world—a world in which each man and woman shall earn more than they use and use no more than they need.

13. The divine principle of hate is not recognized because for two thousand years the divine principle of love has systematically attempted to absorb the race.

14. If it must in fairness be admitted that Southronism is a composition of Pride, Hate, Laziness, Intelligence, and Indulgency, these qualities are so well matched against a Northernism composed of Humility, Love, Industry, Intelligence and Self-denial, that a practical vindication may result, of the Southern ethical and political principles in time to save society, but before the theory has been clearly sketched by the tongue or pen of man.

15. **We** learn by looking, we learn by listening, we learn by talking and reading and writing, and by asking and answering questions; but most of all we learn by working, thinking and living.

16. Under the banners of Episcopal, Presbyterian, and Independent church government, the Christian Church of to-day and to-morrow should be included with one *and only one* efficient minister to each one thousand souls.

17. The theory and practice of all teaching, like the philosophy of education and the conduct of human life in America and in civilized lands, is resting upon these three principles: 1. Health regained, maintained, promoted, transmitted by lives of temperance, exercise and cleanliness; 2. A sense of duty; 3. Industry directed by intelligence upon any proper lines of thought and action which result in that specialty and universality which are best adapted to each individual.

18. No man can really own that which has not proceeded from his own inherent energy, which energy must itself be paid for in nature's only lawful coin, the products of individual toil. Hence all efforts to bestow upon children and citizens the fruits rather than the substance of fortune, **are failures** and worse than failures, because the donee is prevented from that exercise of his powers which can alone develop strength, and the donor, be it state, or friend, or kindred, or parent, is apt to feel that to have a thankless child is to endure agonies of death like those which follow the bite of a deadly serpent. No man ever conferred a benefit who, by reason of this law of nature, did not take the risk of receiving injuries as payment for the same, because gratitude is an emotion of which angelic, not human, beings are susceptible—those rare and noble spirits of whom only one or two sojourn in the earth at one and the same time.

19. The name, "religion", viewed from an etymological stand-point, and meaning to "tie again", represents to the extended vision of the historian, all the glory with which each religion has appeared to its votaries. Religion, in this view, is, in the poet's and in the prophet's eyes, the flower of philosophic freedom, which the **best** intellect and life of the race have produced upon **the** best soil in the most favorable situations of the choicest gardens of human destiny. Religion, in this view, is the rule of reason, which transforms the effete manners and customs of a people into a new conduct of life better adapted to the future than even the old regime was suited to the past.

20. The name, "philosophy", viewed from an etymological stand-point, means the "love of wisdom", and wisdom, in the view of the lexicographer, is "the CHOICE of good ends and of the best means of obtaining them."

21. The name, "poetry", viewed from an etymological

stand-point, means "a creation".
New life and bliss, 'tis this is poesy.
"Poetry is the expression of the best and happiest
minds in their best and happiest moments."

WANDERINGS AND WONDERINGS
By a Wanderer and Wonderer.

Youth was ending; oh! so soon and so fast! Rather
the period of youth, so full of joy, was to last forever,
or be omitted entirely, so quick was the transition from
the hopes and fears of childhood to the thought and
work of manhood, and so joyously was that thought
and labor welcomed and endured! Not without weari-
ness and faintness and sadness in seasons when hope
seemed lost in fruitless effort; but nevertheless joyfully
and peacefully and hopefully were years passed during
which the thought of ages and the duty of centuries
seemed resting upon shoulders made for burdens and
thankful to bear them.

At fourteen years of age our Wonderer lay stretched
in the cradle which rocked his infancy, in the large,
quiet farm-house, amid the wood-lands, where that infancy was passed; and what held him there hour after
hour and day after day? His heart burned within him
as he read the popular story told by a Scotch philoso-
pher and divine about the improvement of society by
the diffusion of knowledge. Playmates at that home
there were few or none, and glimpses of life, child life
and other, away from the enchanted spot, showed the
trinity of weakness, pain and sin in stronger colors than
our Wonderer's tender vision could bear without sympathetic promptings to subdue that living chaos of ignorance and vice and woe, or to be spent in the attempt.
And then, according to the Scotchman's theory, with
knowledge and education as means, came religion, the
maid divine, as an end to which all ordinary means
should be subordinated,- as a millennial harbinger,- as
a guide to a future state of endless bliss, the natural
result of a happy life on earth spent in the society of
christian philosophers.— Such was the dream our
Wonderer dreamed as he held the Scotsman's volumes
and read them in the fourteenth year of his age stretched
in that cradle which was even then but little too small
for him; and the sights and sounds of that dream seemed
like the cradle songs which hovered around the earliest
life of that child, seemed like the smiles and sunlight
and beautiful world which opened to the earliest vision
of that healthy infant awaking from dreams of paradise
to find the reality more glorious than the dream.

the horizon! There earth and sky, the real and the ideal shall verily meet; for is not that world to be enlightened and evangelized by the torch-bearers of science and holiness? The wonderer must soon become a wanderer and set out upon his wanderings, well content if horse and foot and railway lead not astray his life farther from paths of prudence and safety, than his mental and moral guides lead his mind and heart from the narrow roads of truth and duty. Farewell! home and kindred! playmate and lover! Another Dante treads the infernal shades and purgatorial twilight; and, also the celestial summits, which are brightened by colors more enchanting than morn or sunset but lost in the light of perfect and endless day. No one Virgil nor Beatrice treads by his side nor leads the way; yet the voice of intellect and the vision of beauty never failed to guide our Wanderer in his wanderings.

THE BEAUTIFUL WORLD WITHIN

the horizon! The fire-side and portico and shade-tree hallowed by a father's love and wisdom! The small but long unbroken family circle around the hearth or at the board where father, mother, sister and brother met! The old school-house in the fair fields by the road side! The church and the court-house, the store and the village; the river and the town; the sycamore and the graves its branches covered; the mountain and the brook that flowed through the hollow near it; and—and —pulse of my beating heart, wake! O awake!

"My Mary's asleep by thy murmuring stream;
Flow gently, sweet Afton, disturb not her dream!"

And yet from this scene of bliss, in the morning of life, our Wanderer tore himself again and again, only to return to breathe the divine atmosphere of the natal spot, not in old age and after wanderings over land and sea like the bird fluttering with last strength, to the bough from which it took wing the first time, but after absence of a week, a month, and never more than three months until all the treasures of that horizon were garnered in the bright creation of the Wanderer's own home where balmy love had nestled—until the treasures without and within that Wanderer's horizon, and without and within that Wanderer's soul, had with arms of labor been garnered as the fruit of skill obtained by apprenticeship and wandering and wondering. The Susquehanna river country in the soft air and bright sunshine of May, seemed as near the land of Beulah and the Delectable Mountains as he had ever been, and on the same journey, New York seemed to him like the veritable financial heart which sends its life blood to the remotest parts of the body of this continent; and the river Connecticut and the Yale college buildings and the city of Boston, and the State of Massachusetts in which Emerson and Sumner then lived, seemed to fill the Wanderer's lungs with the atmosphere of Athens breathed in that elder day by Plato, Aristotle, Socrates and Pericles; but the old town of Newmarket where Salyards was then living and where he has since died,— the old court-house in the county town among the Virginia hills and mountains where culture did not deny her wreath to a village lawyer nor eloquence refuse to touch with her coal of fire the lips even of a village politician, nor science and skill withhold the crown of merit from a surgeon and author,— the darling room in the farm-house among the wood-lands, the books, the pen, the grove sacred to thought and song—all these things combined to balance the charms of the beautiful world within the horizon against the beautiful world without the horizon, and for a season at least, to chain the Wanderer with the spell of gentlest, holiest influence, to the township in which he was born.

SOJOURNER AND WANDERER.

Thus early did experience, the safest monitor of man, teach our Wanderer that traveling, except for purposes of science or business, is a mania, and that whoso cannot be a citizen should strive to be a sojourner,— that poverty cometh as upon one that traveleth, and want as an armed man upon him to whom the cumulative advantages of long residence are denied,— that all that people learn by selling their land to see other people's is that each section and people are blessed by nature alike because where something is given something is also taken, and that as the soul is no wanderer so the wise man will earn a home and live in it. Anchored fast by desks and bookcases of his own, with his own press and type to catch each thought which nature and the soul shall send him, without a mortgage on the home that shelters his loved ones and without a cent of debt in the world,— he hopes that his wanderings may be forgotten and that they may cease forever unless they lead him into the wider opportunity which exists in the literary circles of New York or London cities. With hunger and nakedness and debt and poverty—the first-born of the world—he gladly journeys, a pilgrim of eternity though sitting year by year in the same spot, a wanderer in search of liberty. Worthiest sons of men have held the pilgrim's wooden staff which supported an exile's lot; but in free America surely the mind may wander as it pleases on its errands after truth; and the heart may nestle in any spot protected by the constitutions, the laws and the bonny blue flag— in any spot where an honest and holy life can draw food from the soil, wisdom from the air and virtue from the sunlight.

And yet our Wanderer cannot forget his travels as student, as laborer, as editor, as publisher, as teacher; or even as politician! The printer, lawyer, and author

were somewhat chained to a single spot and compelled
to forego the pleasure of wood-land walks and saunter-
ings in green fields listening to the music of birds and
streamlets; yet a little spot of valley and a few miles of
mountain seen from the window amid the hotels and
buildings of the town, and the landscape which would
have delighted the eye of Raphael the Divine, which
looked in upon the little press and its owner when,
in the country, during weary months the art preserv-
ative of all arts was bending to receive the Sojourner's apprenticeship; and the glances from earth to
heaven which aided imagination and reason and the
author's pen in turning thought into form and furnish-
ing habitation for what was, and too often still is, airy
nothingness!—all these views of nature remind the Sojourner of the days when he was a Wanderer and make
him half afraid to become a citizen.

The character of student has always clung to our
Wanderer and Sojourner. Indeed, this of study, has
been the principal business of his life. Place him under
any circumstances short of physical exhaustion produced by too much manual labor, or spiritual exhaustion produced by the worthless and vile company with
which he has frequently been thrown into straits, and
the Wanderer is first of all a Wonderer who requires
countless volumes to do justice to his wonderings—his
dreams no mortal ever dared to dream before.

That study or wonder should have dangers for the
body which bides at home nor looks abroad, may seem
strange; but yet in our Wonderer's case this seems to
be true. The facts are as follows:—

The Wonderer's brother, absent from home, had
asked the wondering brother to take a blind horse from
the pasture at noon, give him water, and put him into
the field again. The studious boy could ill spare time
even for such jobs; because, just then he was reading
up "*The Laws of Life*," and about noon had struck the
story of "Handsome Stupidity", written by Dr. Jackson.
But, taking a light switch in one hand to guide the old,
fat, blooded war horse, our student held the pamphlet
in the other hand as he rode leisurely, without a bridle,
to and from the watering place, when, after re-entering
the field, partly to keep the horse away from the fence
and partly from mischief and thoughtlessness, as the
student rolled off of the horse he tapped the animal
with the switch, and as the youth reached the ground,
the animal tapped him with one of his heels at the side
of the left eye, cutting open the skin and flesh and leav-
ing a mark for life which some one once said resembled
the result of a fist fight about the freedom of the will.

The town may have its cosy firesides and elegant
parlors, but nothing like the balmy air and sunshine
which embalm the recollections of childhood and youth
spent in study, work and play on a farm which was
consecrated by a home of health, peace, plenty and

wisdom,- can so well move the pen, or type, or tongue, or hand in manhood's years amid the madding crowd's ignoble strife.

Even the rudeness of nature and society as it is found in the woods of America, has its charms for the student. Forests falling to give shelter and bread to the rough and bearded foresters, who with all their coarseness are the product of the soil upon which they stand, as really as the trees at their sides: and if these sons of toil cannot bear the sight of a studious form, and are apt to use their feet in imitation of the old war horse,- why go to dead Europe for a more vital and important fact? That fruit which is produced by the wild vigor of nature has the most grateful flavor, and if the flowers of early eastern society can be surpassed in beauty and fragrance by the genius of the new world, then part of the riddle of human destiny is solved.

There was, during an early period, much inclination manifested on the part of certain persons to demonstrate to our Sojourner's satisfaction that he is "better than other people", and should take advice and become a little Mogul in some little home, church, school, profession, &c. This hint not having been taken by Sojourner, the same kind friends and others, and the natural consequences of sitting too long in one spot in old clothes, gazing at sunsets, pages of books, and at the faces of stupid people,- all warned the Sojourner that his sojourning at that point was coming to an end and that in fact he might have to tramp, to wander; that he was "no better than other people", not as good in fact for almost anybody, black or white, could become a good unskilled Laborer.

Our Sojourner was rather fond than otherwise of seeing life from plough-tail, from seedfields and harvest fields, from among the laborers on the public road, and from all kinds of manual labor in which the eye need not be jaundiced by the false colors of foolish theories and practices and need not receive the sickly impressions which natural objects make upon many so-called children of culture. He had for years thus been looking at life in the intervals of study, and when the empire of the father gave way to the empire of reason, at 21 years of age, he made a bundle of a few working clothes and wandered into a county which with its rich land had the reputation of working laborers in harness as horses are worked, and hanging people who said "Nay!" to such a system of labor. The sound of the threshing machine was heard in that land, and though sheaf cutting was amusement for our Wanderer when a proper knife was provided, he had not entered upon this first work of his majority more than five minutes when a gash laid open his left hand almost on a line with his thumb, and the mark is there as plainly as six months afterward although fourteen years have passed away, and there it will remain until the hand itself crumbles into dust—a perpetual reminder that a man may sometimes be more severely punished for trying to do what is right than if he is careless of duties and like a vegetable grows where he is planted and lies where he is thrown. A shout of derision arose from the laborers, a little sympathy was shown by the proprietor, and the Wanderer returned home somewhat discouraged, only to pass the line of his state and read a philosophical dictionary and other similar books whilst his hand healed a little. In less than a week from the time of the accident, he was offering his services to a good old bachelor farmer who had lost a plough-boy. Next morning, one week from the day when, and in a field not two miles distant from the spot where, the injury was received, with a hand still ugly and sore, our Wanderer began to break ground in a twenty acre field which with three horses and a heavy plough and some work at threshing wheat and hauling water, enabled him to sojourn in that section during the dry August of 1872. With a month's wages as a financial basis, and a failure to work efficiently or acceptably in digging a railway cut, he wandered from that county to another, visited a learned Quaker, read his books, enjoyed his conversation and hospitality, completed a journey on foot of 75 miles or more, and then by railway visited the superintendent of schools in another county, refused to teach there, returned again to the old homestead there to remain with books and authorship and farm work three years, until again as laborer in another county he earned the two dollars which were all the money in his pocket when he was married and all he could expect without first earning it for five years and then only $500, his father's legacy.

Surely wandering is ended now! "Staying" or sojourning is in order. Several months passed as day laborer and not then from absolute necessity but from grateful choice, have so far ended the triumph over the Sojourner enjoyed by some little men and women who are weak enough to believe that honest labor defiles honest hands and pollutes noble spirits.— But wandering is not yet over as will be seen when the occupations of printing, publishing, and have been referred to in the Open Letter to Subscribers.

The Teacher is a wanderer, a sojourner. In the days when laws of supply and demand furnished teachers *constant*, remunerative employment. our Sojourner was obliged to sojourn only 4½ months out of 20 before his majority and in spite of dog fights and cat fights for public schools only 6 months out 30 since that time, the first time 3 miles and the second time 40 miles 5 months and 8 miles 1 month, away from home.

But "The Old Runaway" is the successful politician. and the official returns of votes cast in 1879 for candidates for the Virginia legislature, settled the question in time and forever whether or not our Wanderer shall be such a runaway.

Wandering and sojourning, or law, teaching, editing, publishing, laboring electioneering, authorship, and every form of action into which our Wanderer has been led or driven, are only the scaffolding of an edifice which he has been trying to build, viz., his studies or wonderings—social, literary, political, religious, philosophical—and which also by the profane will be called wanderings and passed in contempt or with uncomplimentary emendations.

AN OPEN LETTER TO SUBSCRIBERS
TO
"THE TRIBUNE OF THE PEOPLE."

I started The Tribune in April, 1882. It was then a small four page paper. I enlarged the 2nd number to 8 pages, the 3rd. to 16 pages, the 4th. and 5th. to 24 and 28, and the 6th to 32 pages, when it was reduced to a 24 page pamphlet with heavy colored cover. I had little money to spare for the enterprise and was compelled to print these pamphlets, a page at a time, on a Number 2, Self-inking, Model Press. Nineteen hundred copies of the large 16 page pamphlet, and 1500 copies with pages nearly as large, of the 28 page pamphlet, were printed on this small press.

If I had little money to buy my printing office, I had less mechanical ingenuity than money and no skill nor experience which to use the press and type after I had paid for them. With the help and sympathy of my most dear friend, type-setting, press work, binding and mailing were reduced to an art which did not disown the fraction of skill which blessed our untiring effort.

The duties and labors of a canvasser and publisher fell upon me alone. Several thousand miles of travel over the valley counties, mostly on foot, a trip by rail to Maryland and Pennsylvania, and the active and expert yet fair and just business methods used in canvassing, together with the sympathy and patronage which you, my subscribers and advertisers so cordially extended to me, resulted in the rapid growth of the publication in size and circulation, which (although the pamphlet was published only quarterly), was little short of marvelous, considering the difficulties to be overcome from first to last. Among these difficulties were the spending of money that could ill be spared, as well as the loss of several days' time (on the average) every week and not less than one day any week, and the outlay of labor, care and thought—for the benefit of my law office, which was in Woodstock, three miles from my residence where The Tribune was printed, and which distance gave me a walk of six miles in all weathers, each day the law office was kept open. Besides the necessity of being at my law office each week there were bright eyes and smiling faces at home which more than once brought me home over thirty or fifty miles of railway, out of sections which yielded abundant harvests to the labors of the publisher.

The work which thus piled itself upon the shoulders of one man who was printer, publisher and lawyer, was by no means as difficult as the editorial work, if this one fact is taken into consideration:— For the enterprise to succeed, it was absolutely necessary that the contents of the pamphlet possessed as much vitality and originality as were connected with printing and publishing it and as much more strength and useful invention as possible: Until one interest absorbed every other, original accounts of farms and methods of farming, factories, mechanics, inventors, inventions, manufacturers and manufactured articles, schools and teachers, and items of valley history—all gathered from localities visited—entered into the table of contents Not a line was clipped for any number. In an old mill at Greenmount, Rockingham Co., Va., whilst waiting for the miller, I picked up a Cincinnati paper left on some sacks of grain, and read: "The best teachers of farming are the farmers themselves." Henceforth I filled notebooks with the *talk* of farmers, I taking upon myself the responsibility of the authorship and placing the farmer's name and post-office at the end of his article, which generally contained but a single paragraph. I had lived nearly all my life upon farms, and as I walked with farmers among their buildings, over their fields, or sat by their firesides or on their porticoes, I was able to direct their conversation to such processes, implements, &c., as had proven most valuable in operating upon those portions of the animal, vegetable and mineral kingdoms, which came under their management, not even omitting the proper treatment of laborers and of the farmer's own family and the farmer's demand for good government. The golden apples of law and literature, which my right and left hands were eager to pluck, are naught beside the gems richer than Golconda's which are everywhere waiting for the crown which the farmers of the country will place upon the dead or living head of him who as such editor will do such work well though Homer like he must pass unknown and unnoticed among them and beg his bread. The misfortune will be that the pay will come too soon— that merchants and politicians will convert the author and prophet into a huckster and a partisan. When I visited Chambersburg in 1884, from the knowledge of the country gathered then and in passing over it to Philadelphia and Boston in 1872, I was convinced that The Cumberland Valley alone would contribute a guano sack full of twenty-five cent pieces, ready to be piled on the top of as many which Virginia or any State of the Union in which the farmers are a majority, will contribute to such a work as the Tribune's, well done: because in that field the harvest is dead ripe, and efficient laborers, there are few, or none.

I have long since been conscious that, as editor, printer and publisher of The Tribune, I earned a hundred or a hundred thousand times more money and curses than I received; but I am free to say that I never in so short a time received so large and so certain an income from so small and so uncertain an investment, and this, too, in spite of the fact, that, if I swindled you, my dear patrons, I was also swindled by the large measure with which I measured unto you, and by subscribers who took my paper and never paid for it. My swindling, *if I did* any of it, was the result of circumstances—inability to furnish 32 page pamphlets during each quarter of the 1½ years that the pamphlet was devoted almost exclusively to agriculture. Perhaps some papers were lost in the mails. The post-masters, with perhaps one exception, accorded me the rights which the laws guarantee to the free press. Many persons who paid 10 cents for an 8 page paper received pamphlets which averaged more than 20 pages, and worth 25 cents. Most of my subscribers, who paid 25 cents, the price of *one* year's subscription to the enlarged and improved Tribune, received the paper 1½ and 2 years—value for value, measured on my side in the good old way: a measure, full; the grain, of due weight, of excellent quality. pressed down, heaped up, and running over.— Only in one county and in two small neighborhoods in other counties, did Night come near covering me with her mantle, during my numerous and arduous travels as publisher, before I could find a place to lay my head, on which the frost or dew was falling. I sent my paper in payment for meals and lodging, but in a hundred instances no charge was made; in a dozen cases the paper was so sent under protest, the persons being willing to feed me, lodge me, and pay for the paper, besides.

During the last illness of Mahomet, he said from his pulpit, "Has any one been despoiled of his goods? The little that I possess shall compensate both the principal and the interest of the debt." "Yes," replied a voice from the crowd, "I am entitled to three drams of silver." Mahomet heard the complaint, satisfied the demand, and thanked his creditor for accusing him in this world rather than at the day of judgment.

Gibbon's Decline and Fall of the Roman Empire, chapter, 50.

I often had this item of biography in my mind, since I was unable to print as many 32 page Tribunes as I promised, and furnished 24 page papers instead, because I did not go on and do a work, the importance of which I then felt and still feel, but which I, perhaps, cannot do as well as some other persons. Numbers of the new Tribune, will, if there be no misfortune, sickness, accident, or death, just ahead of us, be sent to such of the few of 500 my subscribers as had a right to expect 32, instead of 24 page pamphlets.

EXTRACTS
FROM
"THE TRIBUNE OF THE PEOPLE."

The Tribune will teach the importance and necessity of Thought and Labor, of temperance and honesty,— of a great deal less smartness and rascality; a great deal more true goodness, real greatness, and noble character. It believes that self-reliance, industry, honesty, temperance, intelligence, make the successful man, measuring success by dollars or otherwise.

Money is not the first fact in anything; not even in money making. If a man only thinks of getting money, no matter how,— that will be the surest way *not* to get money. Labor, skill, and all sterling virtues, must first exist in the man himself, and he must transfer these virtues to his life. *Then*, money follows, as the shadow follows the substance.

Among the farms, as frequently as elsewhere, are found persons to whom that omnipotent dollar is a very impotent dollar. Such people are content with food, raiment, a good name enrolled in the short and simple annals of the neighborhood, and ten, fifty, or one hundred, acres of land which are slowly and surely growing better under their hands. Peace, plenty, and contentment, are the great gain which such people most highly prize.

The labors of some of the best, busiest and longest lives, did not leave a dollar behind them. The graves of men and women whose lives were bliss and whose labors are earth's best treasures, are unmarked and unknown. A hand that is able and willing to work,— a head that can distinguish the true from the false,— a heart which constantly says, "Do right!" and a life of honest industry which earns all it uses and wastes nothing—are worthier "success", than dimes and dollars, and titles and flattery. (Volume II.

A VIEW OF THE SITUATION.

Unfortunately for the people of the United States, politics has become a profession; not a *learned* profession like law or medicine, but a trade as filthy as the scavenger's, as cruel as the butcher's, and as disreputable as the trade of the gambler. Public questions are not viewed in the light of reason. Men whose lives are reckless and whose fortunes are desperate, make platforms to deceive the people who are led by the noses by means of election machines and electioneering machinery. Important questions are settled, not in harmony with the eternal laws and facts which control human existence, but in accordance with the personal and sectional whims, rivalries, and ambition, which for the moment occupy the vantage-ground of public notice and are most active, **not in** deserving, but in *securing*, a favorable public opinion. Yet, whoever speaks or writes, upon moral, social and political questions should endeavor to tell the truth and great masses of the truth, whenever that is possible, and when that is impossible, endeavor to tell no lies and to say "Amen" to no lie, though said lie be spoken by those who wear the livery of heaven and represent all the gold or other brute power of the earth.

The Tariff represents an irrepressible conflict between the Steam Engine and the Plow—between the agricultural and manufacturing systems. Bounties to the North, in the shape of high tariffs, caused one civil war, and may cause others. The farmer wants all the Free Trade he can get and for years he has been unable to get all the Free Trade that he needs. The farmer wants a farmer's tariff, and such a tariff includes Protection of such articles as wool and woolen goods. The manufacturers want nearly all the Protection they can keep, and many of them have grown rich upon the tariff legislation of the last twenty-five years. The South and West represent agricultural populations, agricultural soils, agricultural climates, against the manufacturing climate, manufacturing country, and manufacturing people of New England, New York and Pennsylvania, re-enforced at present by the gold and bonds of Wall Street. A glance at the map of the United States, shows that this state of things cannot last forever, and when Commerce again comes to the help of the Plow, Patriotism must be careful that Yankee Invention and ingenuity and the gold of Wall Street are again ready to protect the nation from the avarice and extortion of foreign manufacturers, and from the scarcity of manufactured articles which might in that case result from foreign or domestic war.— It is abominable that the blood, and brains, and life of the republic, are staked upon an issue, which, at best, involves but the hunting of a little filthy lucre; but the abomination ceases to be quite so great when it is remembered that the whole duty of civilized man is as accurately included in the following formula as in any other:— "Thou shalt not steal; thou shalt not be stolen from."

The Negro is here, for good or evil; for good *and* evil, like the balance of us. The American Idea, which permits all of us to do the best for ourselves that we can do, although we do not do as much good for ourselves as a strong European government does for its subjects—this same American policy presides over the destiny of the Negro, and we have but to watch the results of freedom upon the African race, aiming only to repress vice, promote virtue, dispel ignorance, diffuse knowledge, encourage industry, economy and enterprise. Another view is, that the negro must play second fiddle to the white man, or———go; and another view, still, is, that, "The hapless nigger and his coon dog, will vanish into utmost space."

The Railways must serve the people and not master them; but the people must be careful in appropriating to themselves the earnings of a corporation, for the reason that a monopoly which the effect of sagacity, enterprise, capital, and of effort continued through years of defeat and discouragement, is as really and legally the property of a company as the business of a lawyer or merchant which has been created under similar circumstances.

The **Growth of** Luxury should be repressed in the wealthy cities and districts where it exists, to the end that all citizens may obtain work and such wages for their work as will place within the reach of every deserving person the comforts and necessaries of life. The lion, feeding on flesh, requires a thousand acres to sustain him, and only one good acre is needed to sustain the ox, which feeds on herbs; and yet the ox is the more useful animal. In like manner, one acre well cultivated, will support an honest, temperate and industrious man and his family, while a thousand acres are frequently insufficient to support a drunken, gluttonous, lecherous, ambitious, proud, tyrannical, gambling dandy.

The Township System, which makes the school-house and not the court house the centre of political, social, and intellectual power, is the crowning feature of radical democracy or republicanism; but, unless the experience of the Northern and Western States of the Union demonstrates the wisdom of that polity, the social system of the South should be preserved, because the county may yet be the safest political unit and the perpetuity of free institutions may be found after lapse of time to depend upon a social system divided into classes like those which prevail in the Southern States of the Union.

The Democratic and Republican Parties should understand their history and mission. Grantism and Mahoneism are misrepresentations of Sumnerism and Greeleyism. Land for the landless, or homes for the homeless, and free schools, free libraries, and a post-office practically free to all, are all that are of value in the history of the Republican Party. Local State governments, against centralization, monarchy, and the avarice of traders and manufacturers, are the records of the Democratic party that will live, written though be with the blood of a million of men at the cost of a billion of treasure.

True and False Aristocracies exist alike in the Northern aristocracy of money and in the Southern aristocracy of steel and blood. The real teachers and real governors of the nation should be recognized as they arise where-so-ever they arise, for they and they alone are the morning and the evening stars, the sun and the moon, which measure the days, the nights, the years, and the epochs of a nation's destiny.

Morals are the soul of a free people, and unless they are guarded most vigilantly, freedom is impossible.

Religion must not degenerate into the worship of success in any sphere; because in the face of defeat and failure, its spirit and purpose ever continues to be, the reformation and purification of custom, and the translation into the unmusical language of man of the eternal melodies heard by poets

"Who sung
Divine Ideas below,
Which always find us young,
And always keep us so."

These topics, and such as these, demand the attention of considerate men of all parties. The elective franchise should express a public sentiment which has been purified by good schools, good churches, and especially by a literature with which printing has much less to do than is generally supposed—literature which is a genuine and deadly warfare between all the powers of darkness and of light, as these powers are found in human society and in the human soul; a literature that preserves in the heart of man the undying hope that Good will be victorious over Evil.

SCRAWLS FROM THE WALLS
OF
A THINKER'S WORKSHOP.

1. Virtuous youth is more venerable than vicious age.

2. The seven parts of modern civilized society, are, the court-house, the jail-house, the alms-house, the mad-house, the school-house, the meeting-house, and the dwelling-house.

3. Learning finds its golden age in the past; genius, in the future; virtue, in the present.

4. One woman's heart is worth ten men's heads.

5. Be just and generous before you are "fast" and fashionable.

6. Do not run nor fight too soon when you cannot have your own way: some other people's thoughts, words and deeds may be better than your own.

7. Good foes are the best friends: they put their fingers on our faults and tell us to "Heal those sore places."

8. Dollars can be coined out of the bullion of moral character, and loaves can be baked out of the flour of integrity.

9. All that is on, in, and around, this earth, is sacred.

10. Do not level up nor down to blackguards, and show no more charity than you can.

11. Pigmies are pigmies, though perched on Alps; a spider is a spider, though embalmed in amber.

12. The dignity of human nature is a fiction of the poets.

13. Many orthodox and heterodox creeds, though tenaciously held, are only bad excuses for bad lives.

14. Nature's club preceded and followed the clubs wielded by heterodox writers and speakers, and did the work which the writers and speakers are unable to do.

15. In the small, broken mirror of language, the greatest teachers have pictured to the soul only a half syllable from unspeakable, unimaginable, eternal, infinite Nature.

16. A little enthusiasm is still left in some communities of opinion; but most people inherit their opinions as they do their property—because it is easy, profitable and fashionable so to do.

17. The purposes of ease, profit and fashion answered, most partisans stand on their feet as squarely and firmly as the freest of free thinkers and free actors.

18. Performance, and not pretension, is the index of character.

19. Learning, Genius and Virtue are the offices, and Ignorance, Imbecility and Vice, rattle in every place which the foolish world expects them to fill.

20. The legal, medical and clerical professions fade into thin air, when they touch the possessions of learning, genius and virtue.

21. Order, Economy and Contentment produce Happiness when they cast out the demons of Laziness, Extravagance, Improvidence, and take possession of a life.

STUDENT
AND
TRIBUNE,
VOL. V.
POEMS.

THE MUSE OF SHENANDOAH.

And now to woman's soft white hand
    A holy thing I give;
And with it a divine command,
    Which, oh! obey and live.

Here is a child's most beauteous corse,
    And I can watch no more;
Go, bury it without remorse,
    The Muse of Shenandoah.

Red children of the forest roved
    O'er black's and white's roof-tree;
Of all the vales one most they loved,
    Its name, the child's you see.
Ye queens of song, whose fame of yore,
    Now lives in living eyes,
Inter the muse of Shenandoah,
    The daughter of the skies.

Now Landon from her bower comes;
    A book of verse she brings:
Of woman's love she softly hums;
    Of purest life she sings.
Wilt thou, O morning star of love!
    And first of all these four,
Sing requiem for what above
    Was muse of Shenandoah?

Felicia Hemans next appears;
    The christian's book she holds;
Bedewed with christian mother's tears,
    Her book of poems moulds.
Canst thou, of prayer and creed the slave,
    O spirit born to soar!
Canst seize the spade and fill the grave,
    The muse' of Shenandoah?

The pantheistic Browning walks
    The worlds without, within,
And grandly, solemnly she talks
    Of things that seem a sin.
May'st thou, seer of believing doubt,
    Who lov'st the ocean's roar—
Dar'st raise one shaft at, on, about,
    The muse of Shenandoah?

Wealth, faith and fame have often built
    The Muses' earthly tomb;
The wit, the grace, the truth of guilt,
    As oft have struck time's womb.
Abortions are all poet's past,
    But stars their radiance pour;
This beauteous corse is not the last,
    This muse of Shenandoah.

Mounts, hills and vales of paradise,
    They thrill, are thrilled by song.
Unknown the daughters of the skies,
    They die; their harp unstrung.
From foreign hands, O Harp! receive
    A grave near Ocean's shore!
For thee Sigourney long will grieve,
    O Muse of Shenandoah!

NOTE.— An Indian orator who passed
through this valley years ago, is reported to
have said, "The people of the Shenandoah
Valley live in heaven and don't know it."

"Shenandoah" is an Indian word which,
it is said, means, "Child of the Skies."

THE NORTH AMERICAN REPUBLIC.

The North American Republic woke
And thus the genii of her story spoke.

Columbus said. "O virgin of the west!
Mine own Columbia! How thou art blest!
An orphan child, what perils have been thine!
But only flight can save a maid divine.
Say, in what gloomy glen or cave didst thou
With Alpine mountains wrap thy radiant brow,
And trust the eagles for thy daily food.
And rest in peace, as doth the heavenly brood,
When I from toil and wandering sat down
Within the shadow of a woman's crown
And soon for peoples of the east unfurled
Pure Freedom's banner in the western world!
Which hero, bard, or saint or sage prevailed
In wooing thee, when thou wast so well veiled
From eyes of beastly men? Did cavalier
From English realm, or German pioneer,
Or French adventurer obtain thy love,
And o'er Atlantic billows bid thee move!
Or then did one pure spirit worship thee
And bid thee give a world its liberty!

"Far, far from me, to raise a sound of storm
And ask the hallowed presence of thy form
Forever in my little western world:
For thou hast been and art the image curled
In airy forms around the sun and stars,
Which now and then 'twixt seasons of earth's
             wars,
Doth float in visions of a burning bush
In holy mounts, and when a hermit flush

With youth and truth has dreamed the
world's first dream,
There's naught in nature save the things
which seem
Thine own surpassing strength, and health
and beauty,
Which rouse in him the whole of human duty."

And when the great Columbus ceased to
speak,
Two forms with earthly voices far more weak
Than their strong chieftain's, uttered strangest
words—
For both were men of lore.

The first
Was Thomas Jefferson, and thus he spoke:
"As all men are created equal, free,-
Endowed by nature's hand with rights to life,
To liberty—pursuit of happiness—
So to secure these human rights, the states
Are made by man, for man, and states rule
man
With justice only when just men rule states,
Creating safety, welfare, liberty.
"The name of this Confed'racy shall be
United States of North America.
Each State retains its own State Sovereignty,
Its freedom, independence, every power
Except that named in terms as followeth:—
"United people of united States
To form a more united union,
And to create and execute good laws,
And give posterity its liberties,-
A nation's constitution now ordain.
The senators and representatives
Shall make the nation's laws; the Court
Supreme, construe the nation's laws; the
president
Shall execute the nation's laws. And States
Shall give full credit to each other's acts;
And Congress shall secure good government,
And civil rights, in each and every State."

"Some words of Washington's. 'As
President,
ONCE MORE *I* speak to all my countrymen.
"'You must maintain the nation's sov'reignty,
Main pillar of your Independence Hall.
If e'er internal foes strike this support,
External batteries aim to do the same,-
Teach them the nation's union is for all,-
Your love for it, warm, strong, immutable,-

Your care for it, a jealous anxiousness,—
And your indignant frown at the first dawn
Of each attempt to alienate one state
Or county from the rest, or to make weak
The sacred ties which hold the various parts.'"

The second form:
Charles Sumner: thus he spoke:—
  "The nation's senatorial chairs
Are lofty pulpits in the church of truth,
And the republic's capitolian dome,
A mighty sounding-board; the human race,
The auditors, and the whole western world,
The congregation.
  "The soldiers do not **gain** the greatest
                    victories.
O no, by no means! Not when swords change
                    hands,
Do eagles perch upon the conquerors.
O no, by no means! Not triumphal march,
But promised Laws for man's and woman's
                    Rights,
Have been achieved as victories of war.
Establishment of every human right,
Is consummation of our government,
Without which government is hard to bear.
Free school, free lecture, and free library:
These are companions in the mighty group
Of every civilized democracy.
Each ounce of solace and each pound of strength
Should be a garment or a gem for those
Who, sick, need care, and erring, tenderness."

  "**The** words of Our Good President. 'All
                    men
Are equal. In old Independence Hall
Our fathers said, "We hold self-evident,
These truths." This declaration promise gave
That in our time, weights shall be lifted from
The shoulders of all men: hereafter all
Should have an equal chance."

        "'All persons held as slaves
Shall be henceforward and forever free;
And on this act, believed an act of justice,
Descend, considerate judgment of mankind,
And gracious favor of Almighty God.'"

  The North American Republic *slept;*
It slept, it dreamed, and in its dreams it WEPT.

NOTE.— **Persons who** prefer **so to do, may**
read,

The State

Is made by man, for man, &c.
See page 45.

------◆-◆-◆------

A TOUR
AMONG THE RICH AND POOR.

As the light of the sun
On cold hills of a vale,
Through the clouds that are cold
As the midwinter's gale,
Is the child of vile lust
In the forest of life,
When the man is a wreck
And the woman, a wife.

As the light of the moon
In the murmuring stream,
When the fountains are warm
And the icicles gleam,
Is the fire of the fates
In the furnace of strife,
When the woe of the wicked
With terror is rife.

As the voice of the mountain
When twilight has gone
To the echoes of words
And of times that have flown,
Is the dream of the young
In the evening of age;
But the bright star of hope
Is The Bliss of The Sage.

------◆-◆-◆------

JUDAISM AND CHRISTIANITY.

When Moses sang the morn
Of nature's natal day,
The myths of eld he did adorn
With genius' concentrated ray.
And to the Jewish tribes, forlorn,
From wealth and poverty he came,
And on the ages wrote his name,
By best communing with his God,
By breaking an oppressor's rod,
By giving slaves the liberty,
The laws, the customs of the free;
And, dying in the path he trod,
To kings and prophets yet to be,
Gave birth, gave immortality.

O harp of poesy
Once struck by Judah's sage!
O holy, holiest ecstasy!
O noblest, calmest, purest rage!
Thou soul of wisest prophecy,
That did a heaven to demons bring,
When thy chaste life and muse did sing
Of every lowly duty done,--
Temptations conquered one by one,--
The poor, the sick, the erring loved,--
The rich, the great, the wise reproved:
And, dying like God's Only Son:
One woman friend, one world of foes;--
Triumphant! life from death arose.

THE JEWS' THEOCRACY.

The North American Republic claims
Maternal care from Jews' Theocracy,
Whose cherished sons are Russia, England,
Spain.
The following lines condense prophetic hist'ry
From words of Moses, Jesus and some saints.

O Israel! the Lord our God is ONE.
Bow not, nor kneel to gods of flesh and stone.
Take not the name of thy Lord God in vain.
To life of work and thought and love, add
rest.
And feed thy sires if thou wouldst use their
land.
Let not thy hand nor soul be red with blood.
And do not use that which thou hast not earned.
And be as chaste as God is true and kind.
And do not lie when thou dost speak of man.
And do not lust for wealth, and maids, and fame.

An angel came to Nazareth in Galilee--
Came in and unto Mary, virgin child
Of Judah, saying, "Hail! thou favored one!
The Lord is with thee; thou art ever blest."
And Mary said, "Behold God's handmaiden;
Be it to me according to thy word."
To Judah came the wise men of the east
And said, "Where is the child born king of
Jews?
For we have seen his star and worship him."
That guiding star showed them the humble
home
Where Mary dwelt, and when the young child
there

They saw, they worshipped him, presented
    gifts,
And warned of God, they spake not to the
    king.
 And in those days did John the Baptist
    come,-
He came and preached in Judah's wilderness.
And said "Repent, for homes of bliss do come."
Then Judah and e'en all Jerusalem,
And all of Jordan's region round about,
Went out to him,- in Jordan were baptized.
The people mused if he were Christ or not.
John said, "With water I indeed baptize,
But after me there cometh one whose shoes
I am not worthy to stoop down and touch:
He will baptize you with a soul of fire."
 Then John was killed because he told the
    truth.
 Then Jesus' fame went through the region
    round,
And to the synagogue at Nazareth,
As custom was, he went one sabbath day,
And standing up to read, Jews gave to him
Esaias' book of stirring prophecy.
Now Jesus finds the place and thus he reads:-
"The spirit of the Lord is on me now;
Because he hath anointed me to preach
The law and gospel to the rich and poor,-
With words of peace to heal the broken hearts,
And to the captives preach deliverance,-
Recovering of sight to ignorance.-
Health for the sick and freedom for the slave—
To preach the years God made acceptable."
He shuts the book, sits down, begins to say,
"This scripture waits to be fulfilled to-day."
The Nazarenes rose up and from the hill
Whereon their city stood, they wished to cast
Him headlong down; but passing through the
    midst
Of them, he went his way.
      Capernaum
Of Galilee he taught on sabbath days:-
"The beasts of earth and birds of air have
    homes;
But I have not a place to lay my head.
A man doth find his foes in his own house;
But he that loveth parents more than truth,
And he that loveth kindred more than worth;
Or loveth friends and lovers more than love—
All such shall find the dust, but lose the soul:
For they who speak the truth and do the right
Are fathers, mothers, brothers, sisters—
    friends."

And then to Jesus came an ardent youth
And said, "O seer! what good thing shall I do
That I may have this endless spirit life?
For all the words which Moses gave the Jews
From my youth up I kept. What lack I yet?"
"Go sell that which thou hast; give to the poor;
Then buy thy bliss and be a perfect man."
But when the young man heard these glorious
    words,
Through tears he fled; for he was very rich.
Then Jesus said to those who yet remained,
"No rich man entereth a home of bliss."
    A ruler of the Jews now comes by night.
The ruler said, "Thou hast been sent from God."
Then Jesus said, "Ye must be born again;
For that which has been born of flesh is flesh;
And that which has been born of mind is mind:
For where the wind doth list it there doth blow;
Ye know not whence it comes nor where it goes:
And so are men and nations born of thoughts.
And they who do the truth they love the light:
For light doth show their deeds are wrought
    in God."

"God is a spirit; they that worship him
Must worship him in spirit and in truth."

THE COLUMBIAN COSMOPOLITAN.

EMMAELLA.

And is strength only half as strong as beauty?
  The answer shone within a gem so rare,
  A pearl of worth, a loving maiden fair,
  Whose love had taught, whose life had
    wrought, her duty.
Behold three footprints radiant with delight.
  An orphan, she, she leads an orphan now
  To see the clay that hides his mother's brow.
  While earth shall last this footprint will be
    white.
And now she walks and works where grows
    the thorn,
  Finds luscious berries for the winter's store.
  And then her ax and arm make forest roar—
  An arm whose loss well might a widow
    mourn.
How wise the answer of this woman young!
  "O no! no! no! Girls need not be so strong!"

CLARABEL.

From Beauteous France Belle Forrest came,
  A pledge of human love,
Which Bourbon's name and priestly flame,
  To kill with bondage strove.
Oh! see the vile oppressor's crime,
  For o'er Atlantic wave,
Lives no redresser of her time:
  She's dead and has no grave.

A lover's heart to a father's breast,
  Belle Forrest's mother gave,
And never thought a child so blest
  Would be refused a grave.
In civil war the husband fell;
  His wife sleeps by his side,
And far from them their weeping Belle,
Of want 'mid churches died.

A picture of this venal age
  Is painted for all time,
In which the hero, patriot, sage,
  May well discern the rhyme.
See beauty's form and wisdom's eye,
  Adorning and adorned.
Hear virtue's heart bring forth the sigh
  Which every angel mourned.

"Oh! oh! alas! alas! alas!
  Why must I hunger so?
E'en beasts tread gently on the grass
  Men stamped a child of woe.
In all the world is there no place
  To earn what I must use?
I did my part with every grace
  When I no part could choose."

Deep anguish which will shed no tears,
  Displays pure woman's form,
Above her hopes, above her fears,
  And e'en above the storm.
"God knows, a woman I've not known,
  Nor man of honor seen."
As thus she spoke she did not groan;
  She spoke as woman's queen.

She raised her arm, so rounded, white,
  And partly closed her hand.
It was her soul's last, best delight,
  To wave a lover's wand.
"Good-bye my darling, darling boy!
  I loved you, oh! too well!
I have no grave; you have wealth's joy.
  In death I am your Belle."

She sent one lock of auburn hair,
  Plucked by her dying hand;
And thus did die this maiden fair,
  Far from her native land.
This evil, selfish lover heard,
  But heeded not his wife,-
Unmindful of her dying word
  And a dissector's knife.

SONS AND SIRES.

The morning comes with star of day,
And breezes with the forest play
O'er hill and mountain and the vale;
And while the night with light is pale,
The farmer rises from his bed
And meets his work with hand and head,
And with two hearts which years have wed.

The lab'rer finds his work at dawn,
When strolls a dreamer o'er his lawn,
A poet's soul whose best delight
Is in pure visions of the night
And strongest musings of the day—
In hearing evening's prophets pray,
And reading history's morning gray.

The student, clad in robes of white,
Was waiting for the morning light,
'Mid cedars, pines, and sycamores,
Where sleep the farmer's ancestors.
His brow felt summer's breath so warm,
From garden, orchard, forest, farm;
And him with song the sun did charm.

The sunrise softly pours its rays
Among that grave-yard's hallowed ways,
And there amid three rows of graves,
One flower blooms and tall grass waves,
While through the balmy morning air,
Some heavenly music floated there,
O'er graves, and told of When and Where.

'Tis When and Where, or Time and Earth,
That sing the songs of death and birth,
And though the evening's sunset glow
Doth cause hope's founts to spring and flow,
It is in morning's sunrise pure,
That fame which dared and did endure,
Will own that it is safe and sure.

As sunrise shows three generations'
Desires and thoughts and venerations,
As sunrise doth illuminate
With praise and then calumniate
That which in day doth seem as night,
That which in whiteness is not white,
That which in brightness is not bright;

So sunrise in the common mind
Of wandering, erring human kind,
Shows memories of each and all
With veneration's funeral.
And in the bright imagination,
And in the stronger contemplation,
E'en graves must lose some veneration.

Here in this grave three soldiers rest;
Each soldier's bones upon his breast;
For one small grave, just and no more,
War's fate has given to these four,
Three of whose names must be unknown,
Save as the world's broad patriots own
The cause for which these lives were sown.
But covered well by cedar boughs
And things as sacred to their vows,
Three soldiers sleep the warrior's sleep,
Beneath the breathings loud and deep,
Of one whose name is not unknown
To clay of Old Dominion.

The third of these three generations,
And last of all these populations,
That greet the eye this odorous morn,
And greet the ear with music, torn
From midnight's vision bright and clear,
And noonday's musings doubly dear,
And twilight's watchings with us here:
The son who latest and who last
To death from life's short moment passed
And the old name behind him cast,
Which worn by earliest ancestor,
Who slept beneath this sycamore, .
Is now the common property
Of all this sire's posterity.

NOTE.— The reference to "three soldiers,"
&c., is based upon the re-interment of four Con-
federate soldiers who were buried at different
points on and near a farm in Shenandoah
Co., Va., then owned by Augustin Borden, and
upon which some fighting was done during the
War between the States, (1864). The one whose
name is *not* unknown, is "B. B. Fuqua."

Endurance long has sealed my tongue
With silence for the base and wrong,
And ne'er again may breathe the strain
That in my soul so long has lain.
The soul of Burns again revives.
My fancy soars, it digs, it dives.
Again with hosts my arm now strives.

Methinks I see, I'm sure I hear
Earth's legions coming, far and near,
And as they triumph in their crimes,
A rustic bard doth meet the times
With tongue and pen of lovers' kiss,—
With joys and woes of father's bliss,—
With hopes and fears the patriots miss.

Be strong, ye brave! Be brave, ye pure!
Truth's victories alone endure.
The conquerors of love have known
Joys hidden from behind the throne
Where strength's and beauty's king and
queen,
With countenances most serene,
Discourse of worlds and all between.

When on the Caledonian height
The Muse of Burns was plumed for flight,
'Mid regions of the upper air
And 'mong the virtues, graces, there,—
The armies of the plains below
For once did seem to catch a glow
Of hope for error's overthrow.

The peasants of Auld Scotia's soil,
Inspired by Muses of King Coil,
Ne'er fail to greet th'alarming drum,
And gladden when the foemen come.
The god of Scotland spoke to them
Through lips of Burns. With joy they hymn
Bard's praises,— tyranny condemn;—
And scattered over all the earth
These hardy sons of truth and worth,
To southern climes bring darling north,
And mingle with each home and state.
Which man doth build for time and fate,
And raptures feel in heavens above,
Where breath is bliss and life is love.

LIST OF PAMPHLETS.

Prospectus, 5 pages, published 1876, containing list of pieces since published, unpublished pieces, and a short poem not published elsewhere—"The Christian Home and State."

Essays and Poems, 11 pages. Essays copyrighted in 1872: Health, Education, Religion, Culture, Labor, Life—each chapter condensed into a sentence and the chapters destroyed; Poems copyrighted in 1883: Love and Life, Hymn to Wisdom and Liberty, E Pluribus Unum. Aurora Victora, A Thinker's Workshop, From Youth to Life.

Student and Tribune, Vol. v., Essays, 42 pages:— Government: Methods of Study, "The Majesty of the People", Subjection of Women, Temperance, Puritanism, Strikes, The Curse of the Age, Is there a Remedy?, "The Best Government the World ever Saw", Law for Man and Law for Thing;— "Law": a synopsis including its sources, definitions, divisions, practice theory;— Education: Axioms, What is Teaching?, Common School Idolatry, Examination of Teachers, School Money, Teachers and Teaching, Teachers and Superintendents;— A Freeman's Apprenticeship—Leaflets from a notebook containing thoughts on education, labor, philosophy, religion and literature;- Leaflets, continued;- Wanderings and Wonderings;- An Open Letter to Subscribers to "The Tribune of The People";- Extracts from Tribune, vol. ii.;- A View of The Situation;- Scrawls from the walls of a thinker's workshop. Poems; 12 pages.

A number of "Tribune" vols i. to iv., from 4 to 32 pages.

A Student of English Literature, to contain about 25 pages.

LEMUEL BORDEN, *Attorney at Law*, Woodstock, Shenandoah County, Virginia, Began practice in 1878. Collections, a specialty, and money collected promptly paid over. Deeds &c., written. Titles to lands examined. Written opinions furnished. Verbal advice given. Just claims carefully and energetically litigated, and the litigation of unjust claims as carefully and energetically hindered or opposed, when occasions offer. Prompt attention paid to Business. Small fees in cash preferred to larger ones in promises. Business and Business Correspondence solicited. All letters requiring answers, answered immediately.

www.ingramcontent.com/pod-product-compliance
Lightning Source LLC
Chambersburg PA
CBHW031244260626
47169CB00007B/2442

* 9 7 8 3 3 3 7 1 0 0 5 9 9 *